A SE...

Lucy soon realizes th......................orkshire has been a bad one. As if a new home and a new school aren't enough, the acrimony between her parents intensifies when they learn that a nuclear waste disposal site is proposed for their village. Lucy's mother immediately organizes a group of local women to oppose the dump. But her father fears that the publicity she attracts will jeopardize his career prospects as a librarian.

Lucy befriends 'daft' old Alice Hazelborne, who lives in a tumbledown cottage near Pit Field, the proposed waste site. Dramatically, she discovers that not only does she share Alice's powers of second sight, but that Pit Field was once a burial pit for victims of the Black Death. It's not long before a workman on the site becomes ill, and fear of the Black Death quickly grips the village once again.

This intense, fast-moving novel is written with all the passionate conviction for which Robert Swindells is justly famous.

Robert Swindells left school at the age of fifteen and later joined the Royal Air Force. After his discharge he worked at a variety of jobs before becoming a teacher. He is now a full-time writer and lives on the Yorkshire Moors. His novel, *Brother in the Land* (also published in Plus), won both the Children's Book Award and The Other Award in 1984.

Also by Robert Swindells

BROTHER IN THE LAND

A Serpent's Tooth

by
ROBERT SWINDELLS

Penguin Books

PENGUIN BOOKS

Published by the Penguin Group
27 Wrights Lane, London W8 5TZ, England
Viking Penguin Inc., 40 West 23rd Street, New York, New York 10010, USA
Penguin Books Australia Ltd, Ringwood, Victoria, Australia
Penguin Books Canada Ltd, 2801 John Street, Markham, Ontario, Canada L3R 1B4
Penguin Books (NZ) Ltd, 182–190 Wairau Road, Auckland 10, New Zealand

Penguin Books Ltd, Registered Offices: Harmondsworth, Middlesex, England

First published by Hamish Hamilton Children's Books 1988
Published in Penguin Books 1989
1 3 5 7 9 10 8 6 4 2

Made and printed in Great Britain by
Richard Clay Ltd, Bungay, Suffolk

The weird sisters, hand in hand
Posters of the sea and land
Thus do go about, about;
Thrice to thine, and thrice to mine,
And thrice again, to make up nine.
Peace! The charm's wound up.

WILLIAM SHAKESPEARE, *Macbeth 1.III*

One

WHEN MY GRAN DIED, we found piles and piles of women's magazines in her back bedroom. I flicked through some of them. There used to be this weekly column by someone who called himself "The Man Who Sees". That's a laugh for a start because men see nothing if you ask me. Nowt, as they say in Yorkshire. You go through history and you'll find that a lot of visionaries have been women, and those who were men probably had a woman behind the scenes somewhere, working them.

That first night in Apton Magna I had a dream. You know what it's like when you move house. We'd driven all the way from Bedford to Yorkshire and then spent six hours lugging furniture and other junk around. It was a Sunday – what Dad calls the day of rest, which is a bit of a laugh, considering. By nine o'clock I was shattered.

They'd bought this enormous house, Four Winds,

which used to be the local manor or something. It had six bedrooms, which works out at two each, as well as two bathrooms and about eight downstairs rooms. I don't know why we needed a place that size. When I asked Dad he mumbled something about entertaining so maybe he was planning to turn it into a theatre or something. It was like three ants moving into Wembley Stadium.

Anyway, I was shattered and I went to bed. I had to go up this wide, curving staircase and along about three miles of landing to get to my room. It was a big, square room with a polished wood floor and a high ceiling. There was no carpet, and my single bed and bits of furniture looked lost in it. It reminded me of those rooms they put guests in in horror movies – the sort where you know something horrible's going to happen in the middle of the night. Maybe that's what brought the dream on.

It was a weird dream – more of a nightmare, really. It was dark and I was walking along an unmade road alone. I was coming into Apton Magna though it didn't look anything like Apton Magna. There was just a rough road with little houses on either side, and what looked like a church on a low hill. I think I'd been expecting something good when I reached the village – a bed for the night, perhaps – but the place was deserted. Doors stood half open and the wind whined through black, unglazed windows. A feeling of dread gripped me and I started to run. There was something lying on the ground in front of me and I tried to jump over it, but my feet wouldn't leave the ground and I sort of waded through it. It was a bundle of rags that was hard inside. There was a scraping, rattling sound and when I looked down I saw bones. I screamed. The scream woke me, and I lay in a cold sweat with a voice in my head saying, "Hidden, but here forever".

The scream must have been real, because Mum came in and put the light on. I told her I'd been dreaming and she sat on the bed and held my hand for a bit. I've had bad dreams since I was very small and she's used to it. "It's the move," she murmured. "Finding yourself in a strange room. It's all over now."

It wasn't, though. I knew, and so did she. It never is when I dream.

Two

LIKE I SAID WE DROVE UP FROM BEDFORD. I was born there, in St. Minver Road. I was at Newnham Middle. I had a lot of friends there and we used to have some laughs. We were thirteen and most of us were going on to Pilgrim. I was looking forward to it. There's this nightclub in town, Sweetings, where all the kids go, and I was hoping when I started upper school Mum and Dad might let me go, too.

Then Dad got this job. Deputy Chief Librarian in Bradford, and we left. Just like that. So long, Stephanie. See you, Jane. I won't though, of course. Never.

Bedford. Bradford. Sound practically the same, don't they? No way. Bedford's just the right size. It's got a river running through the middle and a country park. Bradford has no river and it seems to go on forever but I suppose I'll get used to it. I'll have to.

It was a big step up for Dad. Bedford library's quite small, and it's stuck on the end of this big store, Beale's.

4

Bradford Central's a big place with eight floors and its own theatre but it wasn't a step up for me and Mum. Mum was teaching in Bedford but she couldn't find work after we moved. She still hasn't. Not teaching work, I mean. Dad says it's because of the weird causes she gets involved in but I don't think so. I think it's because there's no work up north. Everybody knows that except Dad, and he knows what he wants to know.

He's pretty boring, my dad. He's a librarian, and you'll have noticed there's no video called Conan the Librarian. His dad – my grandad – worked in a shoe factory, but Dad won a scholarship to the grammar school, and this was a very big deal at the time. It meant if he worked hard he wouldn't have to go into the factory like all the other kids. And he did work hard. I know, because he still goes on about it. This all happened in the fifties but he still goes on about it. "I was slogging away at my homework," he says, about a thousand times a week, "when all my mates were playing football or hanging around street corners, smoking woodbines and spitting."

I've tried to picture my dad playing football or spitting on a street corner and I can't do it. He'd have looked a complete prannock. He was one of those lads who are born to wear old-fashioned jackets with a row of pens clipped in the top pocket.

Anyway, this story is supposed to make me work hard so I can end up like him, with a career and a massive house and all that. I'm not, though. No way. All he's done, all his life, is go on courses and sit exams and make good first impressions. He wears suits and brings boring people home to dinner, and Mum has to rush around cleaning and cooking and making herself look nice, because these are important people who can help Dad in his career. I have to eat by myself before they arrive and then stay in my room, and I can't even play my records.

I didn't mean to get on this subject. I'm supposed to be telling all this stuff that happened in the village, but it was Dad's career that brought us there, and all I'm saying is, if that's what it takes to have a career they can stick it, right?

Anyway, if you want to know what happened I'd better start at the beginning, only don't expect a million laughs, okay?

Three

WE'VE BEEN IN APTON MAGNA seven months now, Mum and Dad and me. I go to school in Bradford, which is six miles away. Dad drives me in. Drove me in, I suppose I should say.

I got off to a terrific start at my new school. I mean, really good. Town Park Comprehensive, it's called. Dad dropped me at twenty-five to nine. I walked into the yard and there was this group of older kids hanging round the gate, having a go at the new kids. Pushing them. Laughing at their bags and uniforms and hairdos and stuff – you know what it's like when you change schools. Anyway, I walked in trying to look like I was there last year and this girl – this big, lumpy girl said "Hey up – here's Topham the teacher's pet." God, she was ugly. Really ugly. Her name's Lawrence – Amanda Lawrence, but I didn't know that then.

And then this lad that was with her yelled out, "D'you drop 'em, Topham?" and everybody fell about laughing.

I don't know how they knew who I was. I tried to walk through them but Amanda Lawrence planted herself in front of me so I stopped and said, "I'm no teacher's pet."

She stood with her fists on her hips and sneered in my face. "Oh no, not much you're not. You've only got one for a mother, that's all."

"Well. That doesn't mean—"

"It means you're a creep, and you've a funny way of talking and all. Where d'you come from, eh?"

"Bedford."

"Bedford." She repeated the word in a pathetic bleat that was supposed to sound like me. The others laughed, and one of the lads said, "They haven't got a football team."

"They have, so there."

"Not in t'League."

"So what?" I was getting mad. "Football's not everything. We've got a river and a great nightclub, which is more than you can say for this crummy dump."

Lumpy Lawrence stuck out her jaw. "You calling Bradford a crummy dump?" She pronounced it "Bratford" like all Bradfordians do.

"Yes, I am. It's the crummiest dump I've seen and I've seen some crummy dumps in my time." I hadn't, of course, but they didn't know that.

"Oh yeah?"

"Yes."

I suppose I should have kept my mouth shut but I was too angry. Somebody grabbed me from behind, pinning my arms, and Lawrence drove her fist into my stomach as hard as she could. It was like Rambo hitting you. I doubled up. The lad who was holding me

8

whipped my feet from under me and I fell on the ground, gasping and holding my stomach.

"Blue knickers!" whooped one of the lads. A couple of boots came in and then they ran off.

Terrific. And the fun wasn't over yet, folks. I'd just managed to sit up when a car pulled up and a voice said, "What on earth d'you think you're doing, girl – I might have run you over."

I blinked the tears from my eyes and saw a crabby-looking guy of about fifty leaning out of a Renault. I felt like telling him I was sunbathing – I mean, what did he think I was doing? I got up and started knocking the dust off my skirt. My stomach hurt and I felt sick.

"Somebody threw me down."

I expected him to ask who did it, or why, but he didn't. Not that I'd have told him, even if I'd known. Instead he said, "I'm not very impressed with the beginning you've made here, girl – wallowing in the dirt. I shall keep my eye on you." He looked me up and down and drove on, shaking his head.

There was a tear in the elbow of my cardigan and I couldn't get all the dust off my skirt and socks. I traipsed into school looking like something the dog brought up. In fact I guess you could say I didn't exactly create what Dad would call a good first impression.

Four

"AND HOW DID IT GO AT SCHOOL TODAY, LUCY?"

It was teatime. I'd told Mum all about it already, and then Dad had come in and given us a blow by blow account of his first day at the library, where it seems he'd got the ball rolling and made a good impression and this was no big surprise. Now it was my turn.

"It went okay." I was about to tell him about Amanda Lawrence and all that, but he opened the local rag and started looking through it so I guess he thought I'd gone on long enough. After a minute he said "Hey – listen to this."

It was a piece about some land in the village which this company wanted to bury nuclear waste in. Pit Field, it was called. We'd never heard of it but apparently it was well known to the locals. The company would be coming to Apton Magna in the next few weeks to look at the site and take core samples, whatever they are. It was only a brief item. Dad frowned as he read it out, and when he'd finished he said "I hope this doesn't mean we're going to have fleets of juggernauts roaring back and forth all the time. I bought this house as a sanctuary: a haven, where a busy man can unwind in the evenings and relax at weekends."

Mum looked at him. "Is that all you're concerned about, Phillip?" That's my dad's name. Phillip Attlee Topham, busy man. He gave her the raised eyebrows.

"All? What d'you mean, all? I pay fifty-one thousand for a house that could turn out to be on the edge of a race track for heavy lorries, and you ask is that all I'm concerned about. Well, yes it is, since you ask. What are you concerned about, that's so much more important?"

"Contamination," said Mum. "Radiation. That stuff's deadly, Phillip. It stays dangerous for hundreds of years. If I'd known they were thinking of dumping it on Apton Magna I'd never have agreed to come here."

"They're not dumping it," said Dad in this very patient voice. He does that when he and Mum are arguing – talks to her as though she's about six. "They're burying it. Deep underground. In special containers. That's why they do tests with drills and things – to ensure the suitability of the site. They won't use the place unless it's going to be safe."

"We don't know that, Phillip. Who knows what people will do when there's big money at stake – particularly when the risk is not to them personally but to others – some of whom aren't even born yet. I say this thing's got to be stopped before it starts, and I intend to do something about it."

"Such as what?"

"We'll form a group. An action group."

11

"Who's we? You haven't been here five minutes. You start poking your nose into village affairs and they'll cut it off for you, quick-sticks. Besides, I'm not having my name splashed all over the local press here. I had more than enough of that in Bedford."

"Your name? Your name?" She was getting really mad. "It wouldn't be your name, would it? It'd be mine."

"Don't pretend to be stupid, Margaret. You don't have a name of your own. You're a Topham, and that's my name, and I'll not have it linked with any more of your silly half-baked causes and campaigns."

I ought to explain at this point that my mum's an ist. A feminist, a pacifist, an environmentalist and an activist. These are all connected to isms, and Mum got interested in them when I was small and she was at home looking after me. Dad says it's because she didn't have enough to do but Mum says he's never tried cooking and cleaning and washing and shopping and ironing and making coffee for the health-visitor, all with a sticky toddler under his feet.

Ists are forever at meetings where isms are discussed. Mum was in a lot of groups in Bedford, even though she taught full-time. She helped out in a wholefood co-operative on Saturdays, too. She's one of those people who always have to look in their diaries to see if they're doing anything on such-and-such a night, and they nearly always are. Dad likes to think of himself as busy but he's a two-toed sloth compared to Mum.

When we moved, she lost all that, and the teaching too. There weren't many ists in Apton Magna and if there were isms, they went undiscussed. Mum's not the little wifey type. Keeping the house and garden nice is not her scene, and of course this nuclear waste thing was exactly what she needed. It was bound to lead to clashes with Dad and perhaps she needed those too. I didn't. I like a quiet life. I'm not an ist, you see, and my parents are. I'm stuck in the middle, with a careerist on one side and an activist on the other.

I could see they were working up to one of their really big rows, so I got up from the table and slipped away. I can't stand it when they row. I suppose I thought it'd be different when we moved. I went up to my room and put Queen on really loud so I couldn't hear them. I don't know why people get married, and I certainly can't understand how Mum and Dad got together. Talk about chalk and cheese.

Five

I'VE TOLD YOU ABOUT THE DREAM, which was the first strange thing that happened to me in Apton Magna. There was nothing like it after that until I decided to go and have a look at Pit Field. This was about three weeks after we moved in. Pit Field's where they were thinking of dumping the nuclear waste. Burying it, if you like.

It was a Tuesday, the last week in September. I'd finished my homework and it was a warm, sunny evening, so I thought I'd go for a walk. I said I decided to go to Pit Field, but that's not true, exactly. I just happened to turn right at the bottom of the driveway. If I'd turned left I'd have gone round the double bend into the village. As it was, I was heading for the open country between Apton Magna and Harrogate, eleven miles away. I might have gone on through splashes of sunlight and bars of shadow till the village was far behind, but I hadn't walked more than a few hundred yards when I glanced across the road and saw a narrow lane leading off. It was more like a track, really, because it was unmade – all ruts and potholes. Trees grew densely on both sides and their tops met overhead so that the track seemed to disappear into a tunnel. A sign, half hidden by long grass, said Pitfield Lane.

I crossed over and stood gazing along the dim green tunnel. There wasn't much to see. Further on, the trees thinned out and there was a building of some sort. Mum had walked the full length of the lane with members of AMANDA, which is the name of the group she's started. It stands for Apton Magna Anti Nuclear Dump Action, and Mum's the secretary. Good, eh? She hadn't said much about it at home, though, because of Dad. I decided I'd stroll along myself and see where it led to.

It was still broad daylight but it felt spooky under the trees, and I was quite glad when they thinned out and I was in sunlight again. The building I'd seen was a derelict cottage. There were three of them to the left of the track. Opposite the cottages, beyond a tumble-down drystone wall, lay a big, scrubby-looking field with hummocks and ragwort and thistles, which I guessed was probably Pit Field.

There was a gateway in the wall but no gate. I stood in the opening and looked across the field. The sun was low in the sky and my shadow lay long across the coarse turf; and I don't know why, but a feeling of depression settled over me. It wasn't the thought of the company coming and digging up the field and putting nuclear waste in, because it wasn't a pretty field or anything like that and I didn't really have anything against nuclear waste then. It was just a mood that came on for no reason at all as far as I could see, though I

15

found out later what the cause was and it wasn't anything small, I can tell you.

Anyway, I stood there looking at the weeds and stuff and feeling sad, and suddenly a voice whispered right in my earhole, "Hidden, but here forever". It was the voice I'd heard in my dream. Yes I know it's crazy, but it was.

I spun round and there was this old woman standing about three inches behind me. "Where the heck did you come from?" My heart was going like mad. I can't stand it when people sneak up on me.

"Oh, sorry, love. Did I startle you? I didn't mean to." She looked sorry, too.

"It's okay," I managed. "I thought I was alone that's all. I don't know how I didn't see you coming along the lane."

"I didn't come along the lane." She jerked her head towards the cottages. "I came from there. I live there."

"Oh – I thought they—"

She smiled. "You thought they were ruins. Well, so they are love, and so am I." She laughed wheezily at her own joke.

"What's hidden, but here forever?"

She regarded me narrowly, and I thought I'd offended her so I said, "It's just that—" I broke off.

"It's just that what?"

"Nothing. It's stupid. You'll think I'm crazy."

She shook her head. "No, I won't, love. Not me. Not daft Alice."

"Why d'you call yourself that?"

"It's what they call me in the village. You're new, aren't you?"

"Yes."

16

"Ah. Well, you'll hear soon enough I dare say. We're a sort of legend in Apton Magna, my family. The daft Hazelbornes."

"So you're not alone, then? I mean, I thought you lived alone. I just assumed it."

She smiled. "I live alone, all right. I'm the last. The end of the line. When I say family I mean my father and grandfather and great-grandfather and so on, back hundreds of years. The daft Hazelbornes."

"Why daft?"

She nodded towards the field. The sun was almost down and my shadow stretched nearly halfway across. "Because we won't get shut of this."

"Shut of it?"

"Sell it. We won't sell it."

"This is Pit Field, isn't it?"

"Aye."

"And you mean it's yours – it belongs to your family?"

"Aye. Or it did till a couple of months back."

"Then what?"

"Then the council forced me to sell it to them. Compulsory purchase. My father'd turn in his grave."

"What did you – your family I mean – use the field for?"

"Nowt."

"You didn't keep anything on it — hens or anything?"

"No."

"Then I don't understand. Why keep it?"

"Just to keep it."

I couldn't think of an answer to that. She seemed nice, but I was beginning to understand why they might call her daft Alice. I wanted to ask how much the council gave her for the field but that would have been rude, so I said, "Will the council sell it to those people who want to put nuclear waste here?"

"That's their idea, I reckon. Bury it and forget it. The fools." She looked at me. "Tell me what you were going to say a minute ago."

"Oh." I hesitated, biting my lip and hacking at a lump of turf with the toe of my trainer. "I was going to say I had a dream, that's all." I told her what I remembered of it, including the voice at the end. "And then you come along and say exactly the same thing, in the same voice, and that's what really made me jump." I shrugged. "I told you it was stupid."

"No." She shook her head. "Not stupid. Not stupid at all." She gestured towards the cottages. "Let's go inside and I'll make some tea. It's cold, now that the sun's gone."

I hadn't noticed the sun had gone till she mentioned it. I shivered. "No thanks. I – told my mum I'd be in by dusk." It was a lie, but the place had got to me in broad daylight. I didn't fancy walking back through that tunnel of trees in the dark.

The old woman nodded. "You'd best get on, then, only remember – Alice'd be pleased if you stopped by sometime for a cup and a chat." She turned and began walking slowly across the track. "There aren't many of us left."

I wanted to follow her and ask her what she meant by that, but I knew if I did she'd have me in for that cup of tea and it'd be properly dark by the time I got away. I called after her. "I'll come Saturday if I can. In the afternoon."

18

She gave no sign of having heard me. I stood watching till she reached her door but she went in and closed it without a glance in my direction and I wondered again if I'd offended her. If so, she'd have to lump it. At least I'd found out which cottage was hers. It didn't look much different from the other two and I didn't really fancy visiting her in it. Well – I needn't if I didn't want to.

I turned and started walking quickly in the very middle of the track with my head down and my hands in my pockets. It was almost dark under the trees and this, together with the roughness of the road, reminded me of my dream. I'd got about halfway when I glanced back and saw two men pushing a handcart. What light there was was behind them, so they were silhouetted against it and I couldn't tell which way they were going, but since we hadn't passed each other I assumed we were heading in the same direction. I don't know why, but I didn't want them to catch me and, since their cart was laden and they were obviously struggling I simply put a spurt on, confident of increasing the distance between us. But when I looked back again they'd gone. This scared me, and I was really relieved when I reached the road. I crossed, turned right and hurried on. A car passed me on side-lights, heading for the village, and then a van came round the bend going the other way. They made me feel safe with their noise and I slowed down a bit. I thought about Alice Hazelborne. How could she stand living all alone back there, year in, year out? Poor old thing. No wonder she was daft.

Six

"OH, MY GOD!"

It was Wednesday teatime and Dad was reading the paper. He brings it home from the library so it doesn't cost us anything. Big deal.

"What is it, Phillip?" asked Mum, who knew very well what it was. Here we go again, I thought.

"This, of course." He turned the paper so that we could see the photo of Mum he'd found.

"The caption reads "Ms Linsey," and the item refers to you as Ms Linsey throughout. I suppose you gave them your maiden name because of what I said about mine, but they've mentioned this address, so everybody will be wondering why you and I have different names. They'll think we're not married. I don't suppose that occurred to you, did it?"

Mum nodded. "It occurred to me, yes. But if as you said I'm not to use your name, what alternative have I?"

"You had the very practical alternative of not starting

this nonsense in the first place. What the devil does AMANDA mean, anyway?"

"Apton Magna Anti Nuclear Dump Action," said Mum, placidly. "May I see, please?" She held out her hand for the paper and Dad thrust it at her. His face was very red. Mum was obviously delighted with the piece and started reading bits out. I concentrated on my plate.

"Secretary Margaret Linsey told our reporter: 'The people of Apton Magna aren't fools. They know how deadly nuclear waste is, and they won't stand idly by while their village is contaminated for all time by this proposed dump. If NERDS think they're going to ride roughshod over our wishes then they'd better think again.'"

"NERDS?" whispered Dad, picking at the edge of his place mat.

Mum nodded. "Nuclear Effluent Recycling and Disposal Services. That's the name of the outfit, and a most appropriate one, in my opinion." She slapped the open paper. "This'll do us a lot of good, y'know – no such thing as bad publicity and all that."

Dad chewed his bottom lip. He was trying to keep his temper. Mum can be quite tactless at times. "There may be no such thing as bad publicity for you, but if you think all this will have no adverse effect on my career you're mad. I shouldn't be surprised if the powers that be are wondering at this moment who this woman is I'm shacked up with."

He got up so violently that his chair fell over. "I honestly wonder sometimes why I bother." He went and stood by the window, gazing out with his fists clenched in his trouser pockets.

Mum spoke to his back. "I don't care what the powers that be, as you call them, are wondering. If this stuff is dumped here, and there's a leak or an accident of some sort, the powers that be will not come within a hundred miles of this place. They'll seal it off, and we'll all be dead."

I didn't ask to leave the table. My appetite had gone anyway, so I got up and left. I went upstairs and shut myself in my room and lay on the bed, listening to local radio through headphones to block the pair of them out. Domestic bliss? You can keep it.

Seven

IT DIDN'T END THERE, of course. Thursday morning we had a silent breakfast. I don't know if you've ever sat through one of those. You probably have if your parents are together, and if you have you'll know it's even worse than the rowing. They're not speaking, and you daren't say anything either. The tension is electric, as they say in books.

They sit opposite each other making a big thing out of not pouring each other's coffee or passing the marmalade, and you're in the middle pretending not to notice anything's wrong. Sometimes one of them'll try to get at the other through you.

You know – "Your father's in a foul mood this morning, dear – I think perhaps you'd better leave a bit earlier and get the bus." And then he'll say, "Tell your mother that her childish sulking will not prevent my driving you to school as usual."

Oh boy. And then when he's got you to himself in

the car, he'll shove the old poison at you all the way to school. "You mustn't blame your mother, Lucy. She's at that difficult time of life when women tend to become quite unreasonable. We must both be very patient, and remember that nobody can help their hormones." I sit there thinking, what about you, Dad – don't you have hormones or something? But I don't say it. I don't want to take sides. I don't even want to know about it, to be perfectly honest. Why do they involve me in their fights, anyway? I'm me, and they make me puke, the pair of them.

As if that wasn't enough, I got it thrown in my face at school, too. Amanda Lawrence and her gang had a clipping from the paper. They'd been waiting for me, and as soon as I came through the gate old Lawrence flapped this cutting at me and said, "Who's this Linsey bird, then – your dad's fancy woman or what?"

"My mother. It's her maiden name."

"Oh aye – a likely story." This from a boy called Craig Sutton.

"It says here she's been arrested a couple of times at a peace camp," put in Lawrence. "What's it like, Topham, having a criminal for a mother?"

"She's not a criminal, you ugly perv. She's an activist."

"A lesbian more like," said Sutton.

"She's not one of those, either," I retorted. "Else where did I come from?"

"Now you're asking!" cried Lawrence. "I think you came out of a flamin' test-tube, kid. I reckon you were an experiment."

"Aye," sneered Sutton. "A failed experiment and all."

"A mutant," suggested another lad, and Sutton added, "What's your mum scared of, Topham – does she think the radiation'll turn you both normal?"

Everybody laughed, and if the buzzer hadn't gone at that moment for start of school I guess I'd have been duffed up again.

It still wasn't over, either. You remember the old guy who nearly drove his car over me? Well, his name's Mr. Airey and I have him for history. I've always been lucky like that. Anyway, it was history that afternoon, and as soon as we'd all got settled he said, "I see from the local press that somebody's mother – I assume it's somebody's mother – is bent on making a little history of her own." He said it with a sort of smirk, and a titter went round the class. Lovely Lawrence and her bunch weren't in my set, but everybody knew what he was talking about. And just in case somebody didn't he looked straight at me and said "Does your mother sit down in the paths of vehicles too, Topham – is that where you get it from?"

I hated him, but there was nothing I could do. I dropped my eyes and murmured "sir" and he moved on. I sat there all through the lesson wishing I'd thought of something good to say, and had the guts to say it. I will, I promised myself, and my fists were clenched under the table. One of these days I will.

Eight

THAT NIGHT I STARTED FEELING AWFUL, and next morning I asked Mum if I could stay off school. She said I could, but when she mentioned it to Dad it caused another argument. The thing was, the company was supposed to be coming that day to begin work at Pit Field, and Mum's group was going to do its best to stop them by sitting down in the lane. Some members were there already in case NERDS arrived early, and Mum was due to join them at half past eight. She'd told Dad the night before, and of course he thought I was taking the day off to join in. "I heard the two of you, whispering on the landing," he said.

"It had nothing to do with the blockade," Mum told him. "The child's unwell."

Child. Anyway, he gave in and went off to Bradford alone, but I could tell he didn't believe us.

I didn't join in. I wasn't all that bothered then, and

anyway I really was unwell. Mum went of course, and she told me all about it when she got back around one o'clock.

The company arrived at ten, with a van and a long yellow truck with some sort of drilling equipment on it. The van turned into Pitfield Lane and the driver found himself bearing down on fifteen women and men who were sitting or lying on the track in front of a barricade of branches and various bits of rubbish they'd found in the woods. He braked and got out. Mum said you could tell by his face he'd seen it all before. The truck had started to turn but couldn't get all the way round because of the van. It stopped with its back end sticking out into the main road. Passing vehicles were having to swerve to get past. The van driver lit a cigarette, gazed at the blockaders for a moment then strolled back and started talking to his colleague in the truck. After a minute he climbed down from his cab and the two of them advanced unhurriedly, smoking.

"Who's in charge?" asked the van driver. Nobody answered and he asked again, more loudly. "Who's in charge?"

Mum, who was sitting cross-legged in the middle of the track, said, "I'm secretary of the group – will I do?" The two men stared down at her, stonily.

"Get these people off the road, love," said the van driver. "They'll have to move sooner or later, and it might as well be sooner."

"I don't agree," said Mum. "We're defending our village. This is our home, and our children's home, and we will not have it contaminated."

The man sighed. "You people are all alike. You'll move when the police get here."

"No we won't," said Mum, and there were murmurs of support from those around her. The two men withdrew a few yards, whispered together and then split up. The van driver advanced again while the other man walked back to his truck.

"My mate's calling our base on radio," he said. "They'll call the police. We're used to handling situations like this."

"Bully for you," said Mum. "The local press'll be here soon to watch how you handle us."

The truck's engine started and its driver began backing it out of the lane, guided by a third man who must have been riding with him. "Look!" cried Mum. "They're retreating. One-nil to us." The blockaders cheered and waved as the truck withdrew. The van driver eyed them sourly.

"He's parking in the side," he growled. "That's all." He seemed uncomfortable, avoiding the eyes of the protestors and looking every few seconds to see if his mate was coming back yet.

To increase his discomfiture, Mum and the others started singing. They held hands and swayed from side to side as they sang. The man was embarrassed. He drew a pattern in the dust with the toe of his shoe, pretending to be absorbed by it. Then he stood with his hands behind his back and his feet apart and stared over their heads with a serious expression on his face. Finally he turned and, as casually as he could manage, sauntered back to his van, leaned on it and lit another cigarette.

After about ten minutes his mate reappeared and said something to him. The two of them gazed towards the protestors, who were still singing. Then the van driver got in his van and started it, his mate helped him back out of the lane and both vehicles were driven off.

Naturally, the protestors were over the moon. "High" is Mum's word for it. She was still high when she got home. "They'll be back of course," she said. "But we win round one. And a chap showed up from the local rag. NERDS had gone by then but he talked to us and took some pictures and he says it'll be in tonight. And next time I bet we'll have the nationals there, and the T.V. people, too." She was breathless and her eyes shone and I did my best to look pleased, but I couldn't help wishing she'd asked if I felt better.

Nine

ALL HELL BROKE LOOSE when Dad got home with the paper. He threw it on the table and it knocked over the sauce-boat. There was mint sauce everywhere.

"You needn't think I'm cleaning it up!" cried Mum.

"Well I'm certainly not!" yelled Dad. "And I don't want any dinner either." He slammed off to his study.

Mum rescued the paper from a green puddle, dabbed it with a paper towel and sat reading while I dashed around draining potatoes and trying to keep the chops from burning.

They'd got the main headline. "Protestors Foil Pit Field Probe', it said. There was a picture of the group, grinning and making thumbs-up signs into the camera, and two columns of stuff. Mum was described as "secretary and spokesperson", which pleased her, and as "wife of Bradford's recently appointed Deputy Chief Librarian", which did not.

We ate, the two of us, while Dad sulked in his room.

The chops were singed, the spuds were mushy and all the sauce had soaked into the tablecloth but Mum chatted on, high as a kite, till I just happened to remark that perhaps it was a bit rough on Dad that the paper had mentioned him when he had nothing to do with it. I got a lecture then about how society always defines women in terms of their husbands, and that it was rough on her, not him. "It's for you that we're doing what we're doing," she said. "You and your generation, and I would have thought the least you could do was to refrain from taking sides against me."

I didn't know what to say, so I didn't say anything. We finished the meal in silence and then I mumbled something about feeling rough and went up to my room. So there we were. Three people in a great big house, separated from one another by something more than walls and empty space.

Ten

I'D HALF PROMISED ALICE HAZELBORNE I'd visit her
Saturday, so after a morning of minimal communica-
tion and awkward silences I set off. It was a warm day
and there was a lot of traffic on the road, heading for
the coast. I was glad to get away from it when I finally
managed to cross.

It was pleasantly cool under the trees. Two middle-
aged people, a woman and a man, were sitting in canvas
chairs near a makeshift barricade. The woman rose as I
approached. She smiled.

"Hello. You're Lucy, aren't you?"

"Yes."

She stuck out a hand. "Pleased to meet you. I'm
Mabel. Friend of your mother's. And this is Tom."

Tom got out of his chair and shook my hand too.
"Come to join us have you, Lucy?"

I shook my head. "No. I'm on my way to see Ms
Hazelborne."

"Daft Alice?" Tom gave me a quizzical look. "How on earth d'you come to know old Alice?"

"We met the other day. Tuesday. I was looking at Pit Field and she came out and we got talking."

"What did she say?"

"Oh, a few things. Pit Field was hers, wasn't it?"

"Yes it was. What else did she tell you?" He chuckled. "You don't want to take too much notice of old Alice, Lucy – she's mad as a hatter, y'know."

"She seemed okay to me."

I must have spoken sharply, because he said "Ouch!" and pretended to draw back. I hadn't intended to be rude, but his remark had stung me for reasons I couldn't have explained.

Mabel said "Good for you, Lucy. He's always saying rude things about my friends, too."

"I'm sorry." I smiled at Tom. "I didn't mean to be rude. It was just—"

"No, no." He held up a hand. "Don't apologise, Lucy. Mabel's right. I'm a rude old so-and-so and there's probably nothing the matter with old Alice that a bit of human companionship wouldn't put right."

"That's what Lucy is, dear," put in Mabel. "A bit of human companionship. So stop talking nonsense and let her get on."

I was about to go round the end of the barricade when I heard a motor, and a Range Rover came bouncing along the track from the direction of the cottages.

"Where the heck's he come from?"

"Manor Farm," said Mabel.

"I didn't know there was a farm on there." So that's where the handcart came from, I told myself. I felt a sense of relief, and realised the thing had been bothering me since Tuesday.

"Oh yes. It's where this lane leads to. It's not a farm now, though. A businessman owns it. Mr. Ogden. He doesn't like us. We have to make a hole in the barricade every time he wants to pass, and he has to wait."

The Range Rover stopped and a man stuck his head out of the window. "Get your infernal rubbish out of the way, will you? I'm in a hurry."

He was wearing a fawn cap and one of those yellow muffler things with red paisley on it. He looked pretty mad.

"Sorry." Tom laid hold of an old mattress which made up the middle part of the barricade. "Hang on a sec and I'll make a way through for you." He began dragging the mattress across the track.

"You'll shift the whole lot this time and leave the way clear, or I'll have the police on you. I don't know what you think you're playing at, anyway."

"We're defending our village," said Mabel, tugging at a dead branch. "Do you know they mean to dump nuclear waste on Pit Field?"

"Of course I know. I can read. And I know what your game is too, and I'm not having it."

"You mean you don't mind having radioactive materials on your doorstep?"

"No, I don't. What I do mind is when a bunch of long-haired cranks starts obstructing a public right of way with piles of rubbish."

"Good clean rubbish, this," panted Mabel, laying her branch in the grass and coming back for more. "Not like the filthy stuff they'll put here if we don't stop them." She wiped a hand across her perspiring face and looked at him. "Do you know that nuclear waste stays lethal for centuries? Not months, or years, but centuries?"

"Don't stand there lecturing me, woman. Get this stuff shifted – I'm in a hurry."

I'd just started to lend a hand when the passenger door opened and this lad got out. I was lugging a big lump of wood and he came over and said, "Here — I'll do that," and took it off me. He was about fifteen, nearly six feet tall with dark, curly hair. He was fantastically good-looking, if you want to know. He carried my lump of wood as if it were a matchstick. In about ten seconds the middle of the track was clear and he went back to the car, wiping his hands down his pants. The feller said something to him as he got in – sounded mad. Then he revved the engine and shot through with his piggy eyes looking straight in front and his face all red.

I gazed after the vehicle. It stopped at the junction while a few cars went by, then swung right and disappeared. "Who was that?" I asked.

"I told you," said Mabel. "Mr. Ogden. Lovely, isn't he?"

"No, I don't mean him. I mean the lad."

"That's his son, Tim. He seems a decent kid. Takes after his mother, I suppose."

Decent kid. Only knocked me sideways, that's all. They were building the barricade again. I helped, but I was mooning so much I didn't notice what I was doing. Tim. Tim Ogden. Timothy Ogden. "I don't know why we're doing this," I said. "They'll probably be back in ten minutes."

"You hope," said Mabel. So it was showing. So what?

They didn't come back, though. When the track was blocked again I said so long to Mabel and Tom and went on.

The old woman seemed pleased to see me. She fussed around, getting me settled and putting the kettle on. Her place was a real dump. I was sitting in this dim, cluttered little room with a wood fire and stuffing coming out of the chair. The walls had dark little pictures in thick frames, and were so dirty you couldn't tell whether they were papered or painted. The carpet had holes here and there and felt sticky under your shoes. In front of the fire an ancient-looking cat slept on a tatty rug. There was a great black sideboard or dresser with a glass dome of stuffed birds on it. The glass was milky-grey with dust and the whole place ponged like the inside of a very old running shoe.

"Tea'll be ready in a jiffy, love." It was a pretty long jiffy because she didn't have a proper kettle. There was an iron stand over the fire and one of those big, black kettles on it with a long spout like you see in nursery-rhyme books. Polly put the kettle on. She didn't have teabags, either. She got this wooden box off the dresser and scooped tea from it into a big brown teapot. When the kettle finally boiled she lifted it off with a dishcloth and filled the pot. She stirred it before putting the lid on. She poured the tea through a strainer to catch the leaves. "There," she said, handing mine to me. I wondered how long it had been since the cup was last used, and hoped it wasn't as dusty as the glass dome.

She was a funny looking woman, old Alice. She'd a big, hooky nose and almost no chin, so that when you saw her sideways her face looked like a hawk's – like that Egyptian god with a hawk's head if you've ever seen him. She had on the same clothes she'd worn on Tuesday – a flowered, wrap-around pinny thing over a grey dress, thick wrinkled stockings and these ancient slippers with the soles hanging off. She was fantastically thin – heron's legs to go with her hawk's face – and she had this straight, very fine white hair that came down to her shoulders. She wasn't dirty – I mean she must have washed that hair every day – but what I'm saying is her clothes were old and shabby and they'd never use her house to shoot a Persil ad in.

Anyway, she sat down opposite me and I said, "What did you mean when you said there aren't many of us left?"

She sipped her tea, looking at me through the steam. After a bit she lowered her cup and, instead of answering said, "What's your name, love?"

"Lucy." I'd forgotten I hadn't told her on Tuesday. "Lucy Topham."

"Ah-ha. How old are you, Lucy?"

"Thirteen. I'll be fourteen in four weeks. October thirty-first."

"Hmm. Wish I could say the same." She looked about her, took another sip of tea and shook her head. "No, I don't – not really." She sounded sad and I wondered how many days she'd spent alone in this dark little room.

"What did you mean?" I pursued. This time she said, "Your dream, Lucy. The one you told me about. You know it wasn't just a dream, don't you – that there was a meaning behind it?"

"I think so. I mean, I've had dreams before, and

they've sort of come true, but then I've had others that haven't. Once, when I was about four, I dreamt that my gran's silver thimble was down inside her sofa, and when we went to her house I showed her and she put her hand down and it was. She'd lost it months before but I didn't know. She gave me a sweet and said I was a clever girl but her and Mum gave each other a funny look when they thought I wasn't looking."

"And there've been other times?"

"Yes. They're not always nice like that one. A couple of years ago I dreamt I saw a man under the sea, dead. His eyes were open. I woke up screaming and my mum came in and I told her. A few weeks later my Uncle Bernard drowned in a boating accident near Ramsgate. He was Mum's brother."

Alice, gazing into her teacup, nodded. "I dream too, Lucy, and sometimes mine come true, and that's why I said there aren't many of us left. People who see, I mean. People like you and me."

Talking about all this weird stuff reminded me of what I'd seen after I left her Tuesday and I said, "I suppose it's Mr. Ogden and his son who push stuff around on a handcart?"

"Handcart?"

"Yes. I saw them when I was going home Tuesday. Under the trees."

"Ah."

"They looked as if they had a real load on. What do they want to use a contraption like that for when they've got a Range Rover?"

"It wasn't them you saw, love. It was – somebody else."

"Who? And where were they going?"

Alice smiled and shook her head. "Who indeed, Lucy, and where. And when, for that matter."

"I told you when. Tuesday."

"A Tuesday, perhaps. Some Tuesday, long ago. Hidden, but here forever."

"You mean—?"

She nodded. "I'm afraid so, love. I see them sometimes myself."

"Sweet Jesus." I gulped my tea. The cup rattled when I put it in the saucer. I'd always tried to tell myself the whole thing was rubbish, dreams and ghosts and all that – just a series of coincidences. After all, I'd dreamt of a wolf in my wardrobe when I was small and there was no wolf in there. At least I don't suppose there was.

"What d'you think my dream meant?" I asked, after a pause.

Alice shrugged. I don't know, Lucy. We shall have to wait and see what happens."

"But if my dream was a warning of some sort, shouldn't we be doing something about it? I mean, if I'd recognised the drowned man as my Uncle Bernard, we could have warned him not to go sailing and he'd be alive now, wouldn't he?"

Alice shook her head. "I doubt it, Lucy. It's getting people to believe, you see. An ancestor of mine – I'm going back a long way now – dreamt that a terrible sickness was coming to the village and that people would die if they didn't flee. She tried to tell them, and they laughed at her. When she persisted they called her a witch, and that stilled her tongue because they used to kill witches in those days and she was afraid. The

39

people stayed here, and when the sickness came hundreds died."

"So they knew she'd been right all along?"

"Aye – and do you know how they made up for not having believed her?"

"How?"

"They hanged her. Said she'd brought the plague on the village with her magic. The tree they hanged her from was still standing in my grandfather's time."

"But that's not fair," I cried. "She'd tried to save them."

Alice nodded. "They didn't believe, you see. If it'd been now, they wouldn't have hanged her. They'd have called her daft Alice, like they do me. Runs in the family, they say. Which it does, only it isn't madness like they think. It's knowing. More tea?"

I shook my head. "No thanks, Alice." I felt myself flush. "I'm sorry – is it all right to call you Alice?"

"'Course it is, love. It's my name, isn't it? You'll probably end up sticking daft in front of it like everybody else."

"No, I won't. Honestly. You don't really think I would, do you – now that we've talked and everything, I mean?"

She smiled. "P'raps not, Lucy. I hope not, anyway." She got up and carried the cups and saucers to a sink under the window.

I stood up. "I'd better be going now. Thanks for the tea."

"You're welcome, love." She opened the door for me. The light hurt my eyes. "Call again, won't you?" she said. "When you're passing?"

"Passing?" I grinned. "There's nowhere to go, past here."

"Isn't there?" Her eyes found mine and my heart kicked as I remembered Tim Ogden.

"D'you think—"

She laid a hand on my arm and smiled. "I told you – we shall just have to wait and see."

Eleven

LOVELY LAWRENCE AND HER SIDE-KICKS had me in a corner the minute I got to school Monday. If I'd been making my own way I'd have pulled the dodge of arriving just as the buzzer went, but with Dad dropping me off I couldn't.

Anyway they got me cornered and there were about seven of them. Lawrence grabbed a handful of my collar.

"Who the heck does your mother think she is, eh? She's not been in the district ten minutes and she's telling everyone what to do. Secretary and spokesperson, my bum. She's nowt but an interfering old bag and she's used my name for her stupid group and all." She turned her head. "Here, Craig – come and hold her while I batter her face in."

I'd heard Lawrence was thinking of being a nurse when she left school and all I can say is, I hope I don't get sick anywhere near her hospital. Craig Sutton and a girl called Tamsin Murgatroyd grabbed an arm each and Florence Nightingale drew back her fist. I kicked out, but then a lad knelt down and wrapped his arms round my legs and that was that. I closed my eyes.

"Hey, you lot – leave her alone, right?"

The hold on my arms and legs slackened. I opened my eyes. Lawrence's fist was still up there like a total eclipse of the sun, but its owner was gaping open-mouthed at the speaker, and unless you're as thick as she is you've probably guessed who it was.

"Let go, Sutton, Murgatroyd. You too, Fowler." They did so, with amazing speed, and Tim Ogden fixed his eyes on Nurse Lawrence. "You can put that fist away, Lawrence," he said, "unless you fancy busting me with it."

You could tell she didn't fancy that at all. She dropped her arm, hissed, "You wait" at me out of the side of her mouth and drifted off with her cronies in tow. Tim came over.

"You all right?"

"Yes." I could feel myself blushing. "That's the second time you've come to my rescue. Thanks."

He shrugged. "All part of the service. I didn't realise you were at this school – when I saw you Saturday, I mean."

"No. I haven't seen you around either. It's a big school."

He stood watching as I tried to straighten my hair and clothes. I was blushing like mad and wishing he wasn't seeing me like this. Lawrence had flung my bag in the corner. To hide my confusion I picked it up and started knocking the dust off it. He stood for a bit and then said "Well – can't stand here all day. Got to grab a smoke before the bell goes. See you."

43

He went off towards the bike sheds where the kids in the smokers" union sneak their furtive drags, and I gazed after him, wishing I could have thought of something funny or clever to say. Oh, I knew I was being silly. He was a fifth former and I wasn't even fourteen yet. He'll have a girlfriend, I told myself, in the fifth or maybe even the sixth. You needn't think he fancies you, just because he stood and watched you do your hair.

Nevertheless I couldn't help remembering old Alice's mysterious remark of Saturday, and I was still standing there, gawping after him, when the buzzer went.

It won't come as any big surprise that I couldn't stop thinking about Tim. I wasn't in the mood for school anyway, and I did nothing all day. At break I hung around the boys' cloakroom area hoping to catch a glimpse of him but a prefect sent me out. I couldn't eat anything when I got home and Mum was busy writing out a roster or something so I locked myself in my room and lay on the bed with my eyes shut, thinking.

You're crazy, I told myself. Crazy. You're a kid to him. A little kid. He probably feels the same way Lawrence does about Mum and AMANDA and all that. He helped you Saturday because he was in a hurry, and he rescued you today because he likes to throw his weight around. And that's it. That's all there is to it.

It was no good, though. I kept thinking about Alice Hazelborne, who knew things, and who said "Isn't there?" when I told her there was nowhere for me to go beyond her cottage. She couldn't know I'd taken a fancy to Tim Ogden, could she? Or could she? I recalled that Mabel had spotted it easily enough. Maybe Alice had seen what happened at the barricade and deduced something from my face or manner when I drank tea with her. Maybe. But wasn't it just as likely she'd had a dream about me and Tim? They call her daft Alice, I reminded myself. Daft Alice who whispers bits of rubbish in your ear. Tom had warned me not to take her too seriously.

I lay there torturing myself like that for ages. Dad knocked once and tried my door but I didn't respond and he went away. It got dark. I hadn't done my homework. I couldn't be bothered with it. When I went to bed I couldn't sleep and of course the dream I'd hoped for never came. They say that falling in love is wonderful. That's out of an old song, and the guy that wrote it didn't know what he was on about.

Twelve

NEXT DAY WAS SOMETHING ELSE. A red letter day. The day I wrecked my life and found a friend. It happened like this.

The homework I hadn't done was for Mrs. Baverstock, the biology teacher. She's got a reputation for being really strict and a lot of the kids are nervous of her so she's not used to people missing out on homework. You're supposed to find her or stick it in her pigeon hole outside the staffroom. Anyway, I got a message to see her in her room at twelve o'clock.

I wasn't looking forward to it. Baverstock's a shouter, and at least half the kids on detention on any given day are likely to be there because of her.

Anyway, at twelve o'clock I went along to her room and there was another girl standing outside her door. She was a black girl about the same age as me. I'd seen her around, but we didn't have any classes together. I gave her a smile. "Hi."

"Hi." She smiled back.

"Have you knocked?"

She nodded. "I think she's got a class."

"It's after twelve."

"You know old Baverstock."

"Yes, worse luck. I'm here for homework."

"Me too. I was baby-sitting for my sister last night."

"I don't even have that excuse. I couldn't be bothered."

The girl laughed. "Better not tell Baverstock that."

"No way. D'you think I should knock?"

"No. Kids'll be out any time. What they call you?"

"Lucy."

"I'm Maudlyn."

"Hi."

"Hi."

There was a shy interlude after that. We'd run out of things to say and we avoided each other's eyes. It didn't last long, because the door burst open and kids poured out like a jailbreak. Old Baverstock came hot on their heels shouting "Don't run!" as they clattered off down the corridor. Then she saw Maudlyn and me and said, "Hmm. Well, don't skulk about in the corridor. And you'd better have very good excuses, the pair of you."

She didn't like Maudlyn's. "Baby-sitting, Davis? For your sister? And I suppose that's a lot more important than your education?"

"Please, Miss—"

"That's what you plan to be when you leave school is it – a baby-sitter?"

"No, Miss."

"Then why do it? Why put it before your home-work, eh?"

"Please, Miss, I took it with me but the baby wouldn't go to sleep. I had to nurse him all night."

"My heart bleeds for you, Davis. You'll report here at three forty-five, with your assignment, and you'll stay here till it's done to my satisfaction. Is that clear?"

"Yes, Miss." As she traipsed past me, Maudlyn winked and smiled and I smiled back.

"What are you grinning at, girl?"

"N-nothing Miss."

"D'you know what they do with persons who grin at nothing?"

"No, Miss."

"You soon will, if you carry on doing it. I suppose you were sitting with somebody's baby too?"

"No, Miss." I hadn't thought up an excuse and I could hardly tell her I'd spent the evening fantasising over one of the lads in the fifth form.

"Well?"

"Please, Miss, I couldn't be bothered."

I don't know why I said it. I was vaguely aware of Maudlyn loitering by the door and perhaps I wanted to impress her or give her a laugh. Anyway the words were out and nothing could bring them back.

Mrs. Baverstock flinched. "What?" Her voice for once was soft – barely audible. "What was that you said?"

"Nothing, Miss." Sounds of stifled mirth reached me from the corridor but I wasn't laughing.

"You couldn't be bothered. That is what you said, isn't it, Topham?"

I nodded dumbly.

"Very well. Since you can't be bothered doing the homework I set you, I shall set you no more. I will write to your parents, giving the reason for my decision. They'll be none too pleased, I fancy."

Pleased? Oh sure, they'd love it. Coming on top of everything else it'd really make their day. Especially Dad, who used to do his homework while all his mates spat and smoked on street corners. I stood gaping at old Baverstock and I couldn't believe I'd said what I'd said to her.

She stared back, cold as ice. "That'll be all, Topham."

In the corridor I got a gleeful squeeze from Maudlyn. "Fantastic!" she squealed. Her face was wet where she'd cried laughing. "I bet no one's ever said anything like that to Baverstock before – you're ever so brave."

"Ever so stupid, you mean. She's writing to my parents. Dad'll go ape-shape."

"It was worth it, though, wasn't it? Her face."

"You don't know my dad."

"It'll be okay." She wiped her cheeks with her palm. "I can't wait to tell everybody."

"It's all right for you," I said.

Thirteen

THERE WAS NOTHING IN THE POST WEDNESDAY. I heard
the mail drop while we were finishing breakfast and
jumped up to fetch it. I had this mad idea that if there
was an envelope with Baverstock's writing on it I'd
stuff it in my pocket and Mum and Dad would be none
the wiser, but there wasn't. Maybe she's forgotten, I
thought, but I knew I was clutching at straws.

So, first the good news. When I got to school
Maudlyn was waiting by the gate. She smiled as I got
out of the car. It felt nice to have a friend, and sad, too,
because it reminded me of Jane and Stephanie back in
Bedford.

And it wasn't only Maudlyn. Kids seemed friendlier
all round. Suddenly I was getting smiles, and the odd
"Hi". Even Lawrence didn't bother me, so the story
must have got around. I began to feel it'd been worth it,
after all.

The letter came Thursday. The old bag hadn't wasted

a first-class stamp on me. I recognised her writing when Dad dropped the envelope on the table. He always sorts the mail into two piles before he opens anything — a boring pile with bills, circulars and stuff like that, and an interesting pile of real letters. He put the Baverstock letter on the interesting pile, and that was right, because no matter what was going to happen when he read it, I knew it wouldn't be boring.

I won't go into it. He went mad. He hardly said a word to me driving in, and when we got to school he came in with me and made me apologise to old Baverstock. Then I had to go away while the two of them had a talk, in which she agreed to set me homework and he undertook to see that I did it.

I dreaded my next biology period. I thought she'd really rub it in, but as it turned out she never referred to the episode again, so maybe she isn't one hundred per cent bad. Anyway, that's what you get for mooning over some lad. Who needs it?

Fourteen

FRIDAY EVERYBODY IN AMANDA was supposed to be
at the end of Pitfield Lane at eight thirty a.m. "They
haven't been near since last Friday," said Mum at
breakfast, "and I think they just might try again
today." Dad said nothing and neither did I.

When I got home at half past four Mum looked
upset. "What's up?" I asked.

"AMANDA," she growled. "Twenty-two members
and only seven turned up this morning, after I'd taken
the trouble to phone everyone and ask for a special
effort."

"Did NERDS show up?"

"No, but that's not the point, Lucy. They might
have, and if they had we wouldn't have been enough to
stop them."

"Some people have to work, Mum."

"It's not that. Some of those who don't go out to
work didn't turn up. I'm going to have to call an
emergency meeting."

By the time Dad got home she'd phoned about ten people and was still hard at it. Dinner was on, but it was going to be late and I'd only just started setting the table.

"What's this? Where's your mother?"

"Phoning."

"Who?"

"Her group. There's going to be a meeting."

"Here?"

"I think so."

"Oh, God."

Dinner was a bit strained. The meeting was set for ten in the morning, at our place. "Why here?" asked Dad.

"Size," Mum told him. "We bought the place so that we could have people round, didn't we?"

"For dinner parties, Margaret, not subversive meetings. Anyway, I shan't be here – got something on at the library." He looked at me. "You could come with me, Lucy – have a look round."

I didn't know what to say. I didn't believe him that he had to go in – it was his Saturday off — and I didn't want to look round his boring library anyway. I knew what he was doing, of course. He was avoiding Mum's friends, and he wanted me out of the way in case I got interested in AMANDA. Not that there was much chance of that – neither of my parents was interested in what I did, so why should I be interested in their stuff? When I looked at Mum she shrugged as though she wasn't bothered one way or the other so I said "Okay", but then she gave me a sad look and Dad smiled and I thought this is a war and I'm in no man's land.

Anyway, Saturday rolled round and the library trip turned out a lot better than I expected, because no sooner had Dad left me in General Fiction and gone up to his office than Maudlyn walked in. There's a coffee bar on the second floor and we went up there and spent all morning chatting and looking at lads. It was brilliant.

Fifteen

THAT NIGHT I DREAMT AGAIN. I can't remember much about it but I was in a strange place at night and there were people sneaking about in the dark. I knew something awful was going to happen and I wanted to get away but you know what it's like in dreams – your legs won't do what you want them to. Anyway, it was too late and there was this terrific flash and I woke up. I don't think I screamed because Mum didn't come in and I lay in a cold sweat wondering what it meant: wishing Alice was nearby so I could talk to her.

Next day – Sunday – there was a disaster a few hundred miles away in France. It was on the news. Some terrorists got on to a nuclear waste dump and planted bombs in the earth. When the bombs went off they shattered some containers and released a lot of radioactive particles into the atmosphere. People near the site were expected to die and the wind was carrying fall-out across the country.

It was my dream. I knew it was, and I was scared. I wasn't the only one, either. It was a frightening event, and it woke a lot of people up. Even in Apton Magna.

Sixteen

I WAS DOWN BY THE BIKE SHEDS Monday break talking to Maudlyn when Tim Ogden came up. I'd spent all weekend trying to get him out of my mind. He smiled and said "Hi". We said hi back and I started blushing as usual.

"Fancy coming to a party?" I'd assumed he'd come about something really boring to do with school, and the question took me by surprise. As I stood goggling like a prannock Maudlyn said "What party – where?"

"My place."

"When?"

"November fourth. It's a Wednesday."

"What's it for?" She sounded as suspicious as a parent.

"It's not for anything. It's just a party. My dad'll be away at a conference and we'll have the place to ourselves."

"Who's we?" I was dying to get a word in but Maudlyn's interrogation was going on and on.

"Some of my friends and their friends."

"And us. What sort of party will it be?"

He laughed. "What sorts are there? You know – music, soft lights, grub, booze, dancing – whatever develops."

"No, thanks." It came out really prim, just as I was trying to imagine what it'd be like smooching with him to some slow number in a dimly-lit room. I could have throttled her.

"I might come," I blurted.

Tim grinned. "Good lass."

"I don't know yet though – it's ages. Something might come up."

"It might indeed." He grinned. "I'll pencil you in and get back to you nearer the time. Take care." He shot Maudlyn a scornful glance and stalked off across the yard. Maudlyn looked at me.

"You're mad, Lucy. You don't even know him. He smokes and fights and shows off all the time. He's always in trouble. How d'you know what might happen at this party of his?"

"What can happen? It's just kids from school."

"He didn't say that. He said his friends and their friends. How d'you know who they are, Lucy? They might be a bunch of weirdos for all you know."

"Leave off, Maudlyn – Tim's okay. He's a bit on the wild side, but you're going on as if he's in the Mafia or something."

"Well, it's up to you, but I wouldn't go. I doubt if my mum'd let me anyhow."

"My mum—," I was going to tell her my mum lets me do anything I like but it's not true. It's just that she's so busy a lot of the time she doesn't notice what I do. Anyway, I thought I'd get to go to Tim's party if I wanted to, and I wanted to all right. I just hoped it wouldn't make Maudlyn go off me.

When I got on the bus home, Mum was on it. I sat down next to her. "Where've you been, Mum – what you doing on the bus?"

She told me she'd been arrested and charged with obstruction in Pitfield Lane, where NERDS had turned up at ten to find about sixty villagers sitting on the track. "There were people we'd never seen," she said, her eyes shining. "This French thing's really shaken people up, Lucy. They kept saying 'What if it happened here?' Then your friend Alice came with tea. She must have dished up about forty cups in the end, and people kept popping off to use her lavatory."

"What'll happen to you?"

"I'll appear in court. They'll fine me, and if I refuse to pay they'll send me to prison."

"How long?"

"Oh — a week or two I expect."

"Will you refuse to pay?"

"Probably. It's all good publicity."

"Dad won't like it."

"Dad will have to lump it."

I'd meant to say "There's this party, Mum," but it didn't seem like the ideal time so I looked out the window wondering what Maudlyn would reckon to a friend whose mother was a convict. Good, eh?

Seventeen

THE PAPERS KEPT PRINTING MAPS of France with arrows showing where the fall-out had got to. The dump was near Soissons, about fifty miles from Paris, and a north-west wind was blowing the stuff towards the city. There were articles explaining why such a thing could never happen in Britain, but the maps were on the front page and the articles weren't, and more and more people started showing up to blockade Pitfield Lane. Some of them didn't even live in the area. Mum was in her element. AMANDA made the national press, and nobody was giving me any hassle about it at school anymore.

I didn't see Tim to talk to, but he'd started giving me a wave and a grin whenever I caught his eye about the place, and this was enough to make me feel pretty good. Maudlyn kept wittering on about the party, but she showed no sign of going off me, even when I told her Mum might end up in jail.

The thing that was spoiling it all was home. The rows between Mum and Dad got worse as Mum's campaign took off and her face started appearing in the papers. I was sick of it. Now that things were looking up everywhere else I wanted rid of the hassle. I longed for something to happen which would settle this waste thing one way or the other so we could simmer down and live like other people – be a family, maybe. I mean, I daren't even invite Maudlyn home in case my parents started rowing in front of her.

Well, something happened all right, but it didn't settle anything. There was no sign of NERDS for a couple of days, and then on Thursday night Mabel and Tom – the couple I'd met at the barricade – were having a drink at the Fleece when they noticed this character at the bar. I got all this later from Mum. He was pretty young with a dark grey suit, a Radio Four voice and one of those very thin, expensive briefcases. He was standing people drinks and talking pretty loud and getting quite a crowd round him, and Mabel shushed Tom so she could earwig.

He was going on about his company. It was like every third word was "my company", and it wasn't long before Mabel realised he was talking about NERDS. "My company sees this as a give-and-take situation," he was saying. "Apton Magna helps my company, my company helps Apton Magna. Take your church hall, for example."

"You take it, lad," said one of the locals, and his companions laughed.

"Well, exactly, you see." The young man took a sip of his whisky and twinkled at his audience over the rim of the glass before continuing. "Cold, dim and cheerless. I know. I've seen it. I wouldn't fancy sitting through a two-hour meeting in there on a January evening."

"It's colder than a penguin's bum," growled a voice, and there were noises of assent.

"I can well imagine. So, my company has identified this as an area in which it might do something positive for the village as a token of its appreciation of local people's cooperation." He twinkled again. "Most local people's cooperation, anyway." This dig at the protestors drew sniggers from the men. "We've talked to the Council," he went on, "and have obtained outline approval of my company's plan for a brand new community centre for the village."

A murmur of approval greeted this announcement, and the young man ordered and paid for a fresh round of drinks before raising his glass. "Cheers."

"Aye, lad," murmured the locals, raising theirs and then taking long pulls as their benefactor continued. "The project will be financed entirely by my company and will incorporate a branch library, open six days a week, to replace the present weekly visit you get from the mobile library."

There were murmurs of "Grand' and "About time and all," and the young man sipped and beamed.

"Look at 'em," hissed Mabel. "Lapping it up. He smarms and simpers and twists 'em round his little finger and they think he's their fairy godmother."

"Sssh!" Tom scowled. "Not so loud love – they'll hear you."

"I want them to hear!" she cried, glaring across the room. Some of the men turned to look at her. Mabel stared back while Tom tried to make himself invisible.

"Yes!" she shouted. "It's you I'm talking about. You're pathetic, the lot of you – drinking his beer and grinning as he buys you for his company. Are you completely thick? Don't you realise his company doesn't give a damn about Apton Magna or anybody in it? To them, we're just another crowd of yokels to be won over with smooth words and free ale and they're right, too – we are. What do we care for the future, eh – our children's future? It's free beer tonight and a community centre tomorrow and hey, nonny nonny, all's right with the world. You make me puke."

There was silence for a moment as Mabel stood up and, quivering with anger, snatched her coat from the rack. Then, as she handed Tom his cap with a terse "Come on," the young man said "Please – don't go. This is a democracy after all, and we welcome your opinion – we really do."

"Well, you've got it, haven't you?" snarled Mabel, as Tom jammed his cap on his head and stood up. "Just who are you, anyway? I didn't catch your name."

"Pratt," the young man told her. "Sefton Pratt. Public Relations."

"Well, Mister Sefton Pratt." Tom watched from the doorway as his wife approached the young man and thrust her face to within inches of his. "You can run back to your masters and tell 'em we're not all yokels in Apton Magna. There's some of us see what's going on and we're agin it, d'you hear? Agin it!" She spun on her heel and strode out of the pub with Tom in her wake. I don't know what happened in there after they'd gone but I bet she messed up their little party. More than somewhat, as somebody or other used to say.

Eighteen

NEXT DAY IT WAS MORE OR LESS OFFICIAL because there was a piece in the paper about the community centre and how badly it was needed and how most villagers were enthusiastic about the scheme. I don't know how they reckoned to know how most villagers felt – there hadn't been time to ask them – but anyway there it was, and you could see from Mum's face she'd a pretty fair idea it wasn't going to be good for AMANDA.

That wasn't all, either. That same day the national press headlined some daft story about Princess Di. It was the usual mishmash of speculation and baseless rumour but it ran and ran and did its job, which was to push the radiation story out of the headlines and thus out of people's minds. When Mum went across to Pitfield Lane Sunday morning there were five people, and no more came. Tom was the only man. All the rest had apparently changed their minds. When she came back Sunday night Dad said wasn't it time to admit defeat and she accused him of caring more about the prospect of a library in the village than my safety, and there was another row.

Anyway, it turned out that that was my last day of living normally, if you can call it that, because when I came home from school Monday all set to tackle Mum about Tim's party, she'd gone.

Nineteen

I'D ARRANGED TO MEET Maudlyn in the library coffee bar at seven. I thought if we made it the library, Dad would be less likely to try to stop me. He doesn't like me going out when the nights are drawing in, as he calls it.

Riding home on the bus I thought, I'll tell Mum about the party as soon as I get in, and she can tell Dad. That way it'll be a load off my mind and I'll really be able to enjoy myself tonight.

Anyway, she wasn't there. She'd left a meal all prepared so all I'd have to do was light the gas. The table was set, and there were two envelopes propped against the cruet — one for me and one for Dad. Mine had a note in it which said that some of the women had decided to set up camp in Pitfield Lane and live there till NERDS withdrew. Mum was one of them, and she hoped I'd understand and hadn't waited to discuss the matter with Dad and me first because there was no point. I love you, she'd put at the end.

I stood there with this note in my hand and I thought, no you don't. If you loved me you'd be here and I'd be telling you about the party like I was going to. I looked at the pan of potatoes and the two sad pieces of steak ready for grilling, and I thought about her standing at the sink an hour or so ago, preparing this meal for two, and I wondered if she'd ever be here again. I wanted to run to her but I burst out crying and ran to my room instead.

I was still there, lying on the bed, when Dad came home. I heard the door and his footsteps along the hall and I sat up and dabbed at my face with a tissue. There was a silence, in which I pictured him seeing the envelope and tearing it open and reading Mum's note. I wondered what was in it. After a minute he came to the foot of the stairs and called, "Lucy?"

I didn't answer. I don't know why. I wanted to be quiet I suppose – by myself. I knew he'd start on about Mum and I wouldn't know what to say because I hadn't had time to sort it out in my mind. I felt sorry for him in a way; but it was mostly resentment I felt when he called up the stairs, because of the way he barked my name on a rising inflection, meaning "Were you in on this?" or "What about my meal?" Maybe he was just scared I'd gone too, but that's what it sounded like to me and I wished he'd leave me alone.

He didn't, though. I heard him on the stairs and then he came in without knocking and said, "Oh, there you are. Didn't you hear me calling?"

I shook my head. "No." I don't usually lie. It was the easiest thing to say that's all – the line of least resistance. I didn't feel I could handle resistance right then and he must have known I'd heard him, anyway.

"Do you know your mother's walked out on us, Lucy?"

I nodded. "She left a note for me, too."

"It's ridiculous. She's a wife and mother. She can't just—" He gave a snort of exasperation, crossed to the window and stood with his hands in his pockets, looking down into the garden.

I sat on the edge of the bed with my hands in my lap and stared at the carpet. It was getting dark and I could only just make out the pattern.

I felt sort of numb – as if I wasn't really there and all this was happening to someone else; but something about the way Dad stood silhouetted against the last of the light reminded me of what I'd seen on my way back from Alice's place and I said "It's haunted you know, Pitfield Lane."

"What?" I'd spoken quietly – mumbled almost, and he turned and looked at me in the gloom. "What did you say?"

"Pitfield Lane's haunted. I saw two men pushing a cart but they weren't really there – not now, anyway."

"Are you feeling all right, Lucy?" He must have thought I was rambling because there was real concern in his voice. He came over and laid a hand on my forehead – something he hadn't done since I was very small, and don't ask me why but suddenly I burst into tears, flung my arms round him and buried my face in his thighs.

He was okay about it. I mean, he didn't get irritated and tell me to get a grip of myself like I'd have expected him to. He let me cry myself out, and I even got a peck on my forehead when he said goodnight, though I could tell he felt awkward about it. I felt pretty awkward myself if you want to know the truth.

Other people. They really screw you up.

Twenty

IT WASN'T TILL DAD AND I were getting in the car next morning that I remembered I was supposed to have been meeting Maudlyn at the library the night before. I'd meant to mention Tim's party to Dad on the way in, but instead I sat there worrying about what she'd say. Dad must have assumed my silence had something to do with Mum leaving because he didn't try to make conversation. He didn't even tell me he'd been along to Pitfield Lane after I'd gone to sleep to try to persuade Mum to come home. Maybe he was uncomfortable about our intimacy of the night before. I know I was. We've never been a kiss-and-cuddle family, if you know what I mean.

There was no Maudlyn at the gate. I had to go looking, and when I eventually found her, way over by the sports centre, she laid into me before I'd chance to explain.

"Seven o'clock, we said. I got there at five to and hung around till quarter past eight and you never showed up. Something good on telly, was it?"

"No. My mum—"

"Don't tell me – your mummy wouldn't let you, right?"

"You're not letting me explain."

"What's to explain? You had something better to do, you didn't show up. Why should I care?"

"It wasn't anything like that, Maudlyn – honest. My mum's left home."

"So? My mum's left about six times and my dad's away more than he's there but I don't stand my friends up."

"I was upset, Maudlyn – nothing like this ever happened in my family before. I got into a state and forgot our arrangement, that's all."

All the time we'd been speaking, Maudlyn had been leaning with one shoulder against the sports centre wall, keeping her body half turned away and refusing to look at me. When my voice broke at the end of this explanation she turned her head. Our eyes met and I saw warmth and humour in hers. "Hey," she said, smiling and frowning at the same time, "Married people fight all the time, Lucy. They enjoy it. My dad only married Mum so he wouldn't have to trail over to her place for a fight every day." She grinned. "Now he's fed up fighting with Mum, so every now and then he goes off and fights with this other lady. I 'spect he'll go stay with her for a while soon to save busfare."

I laughed, and then I burst out crying and she came and wrapped her arms round me and I felt something – some sort of force, flowing from her into me and I knew I was going to be able to cope. I can't explain it any better than that, but it was a terrific feeling.

71

Twenty-One

WHEN I GOT TO THE BUS STOP at hometime, Tim was
there. His dad usually picks him up so that I'm the only
kid bussing it to Apton Magna. Anyway there he was,
and I actually plucked up the courage to speak first,
though he had smiled and winked when he saw me
coming.

"No lift today then?" Sparkling stuff.

He shook his head. "Dad's working late."

"Ah."

He looked at me. "Are you definitely okay for my
party?"

"I don't know. I haven't mentioned it to my parents
yet."

"D'you have to?"

"Course."

"So, ask as soon as you get in and let me know
tomorrow, okay?"

"I don't know. My mum's not living at home right now."

I couldn't have told him that to save my life if Maudlyn hadn't lent me some of her strength. His eyebrows went up. "No? Where is she, then?"

"Pitfield Lane. They're camping."

"Ah – that explains something Dad and I noticed this morning – a sort of tent thing at the edge of the trees. It looked as though it was made out of dustbin liners." He grinned. "Dad swore like a trooper. He hates this AMANDA outfit, you know."

"Yes. I was there when he made us shift that barricade, if you remember. How about you?"

"Me?"

"Yes. What do you reckon to the protestors?"

"Oh – I'm not as intolerant as Dad. I think they've got a point, and I'm definitely not keen on having a nuclear waste site a few hundred yards from my home. I hope they win, but I daren't tell Dad that!"

"He sounds a bit like my dad."

"Yes. They should form a group of their own. DAGAND."

"What's that?"

"Dads Against Groups Against Nuclear Dumps."

I giggled, and the bus came while I was trying to think up some good initials of my own. I went upstairs like I always do and Tim followed. "I'd better have the window seat," he said, "because you'll be getting off first."

I let him in and sat down next to him. "I thought I might ride to your stop and go see Mum," I told him. "But on second thoughts I think I'll call home first and get out of this rotten uniform."

73

"Good idea. Need any help with zips or anything?"

"No, I don't!" It was time to hit him with some initials I'd thought up. "How about SPACOP?"

"Go on."

"Some Parents Against Certain Other Parents."

He groaned, and I pretended to be hurt. "I thought it was quite good."

We played this game all the way home, and my stop came far too soon for me. As I got up I said, "Say hello to my mum and tell her I'll be along to see her in half an hour, okay?"

"Sure. I'll ask her about my party while I'm at it."

"Don't you dare. I'll do that."

"Don't forget, then."

"I won't."

I waved as the bus pulled away but he wasn't looking. As I walked to our gate I wondered about his mother. I'd never heard him mention her.

Dad had given me a key that morning. I stuck it in the keyhole and twisted and nothing happened. I jiggled it about and tried again, and then I realised that the door wasn't locked. I went in and there was Mum, coming down the stairs.

"Hello, Lucy – good day at school?"

I nodded. "Have you finished camping, then?"

She shook her head. "No, dear – not until we win. I came for a shower and to collect a few bits and pieces." Her hair was wet and she had a sports bag on her shoulder.

"D'you have to go already? Only I thought we could talk."

74

"I'd as soon not be here when your father gets in, Lucy – you know what he's like."

"He's okay," I said, thinking about last night and because she was hurting me.

"Yes, well. Was there something you particularly wanted to talk to me about, Lucy?"

"No. I just thought we could have a chat, that's all. Like we used to."

I must have looked crestfallen, because she grabbed me and gave me a quick squeeze and then held me at arms' length, gazing into my eyes. "I'm not a million miles away, you know. Five, six hundred yards at the most. And I want you to remember that we're doing it for you – you and your children."

"I'll stay with my children," I said, twisting myself free of her hold.

She looked at me as though I'd slapped her, and there was this big aching lump in my throat and I ran past her and up the stairs so she wouldn't see me crying. She didn't follow, and when I came down half an hour later she'd gone.

Twenty-Two

"MUM WAS HERE," I said, sliding a plate of macaroni cheese in front of Dad before sitting down to tackle my own helping. I can't stand macaroni cheese, especially tinned, but he's always found something ready when he's come in and it'd had to be something quick.

"Hmm. I thought somebody'd been mucking about in the bedroom. What did she say?"

I told him, leaving out the bit about her not wanting to be there when he got in, and he was practically silent throughout the rest of the meal. I put it down to the disgusting food, which always reminds me of this tapeworm we've got in a bottle in the biology lab at school, but I realised later there'd been something on his mind.

When I finished eating I felt sick, so I went out for a breath of air. I wanted to talk to Alice, but I'd have had to pass the camp and I didn't feel I could face Mum so I went the other way, round the double bend into the village.

I walked about a bit, pausing outside the church hall where the youth club meets. Some lads were standing under the lamp in the doorway and I could hear music inside but I'm not the youth club type, and when one of them noticed me and called out, I hurried on.

It was a dark evening, and a bit chilly, too. My sickness had worn off and I should have turned round and gone home, but I didn't fancy trying to make conversation with Dad or sitting alone in my room, so I loitered, looking at shop windows and peering into some of the dark little alleyways that lead off from the main street. Passing one of these, I became aware of a nauseating smell and then I saw that rotten handcart again, parked outside a cottage. I felt myself go cold. It was as though the thing was haunting me – showing up whenever I was alone at night to scare the hell out of me. I was about to hurry on when two figures came out of the cottage, carrying something between them. They swung whatever it was onto the cart and stood, wiping their hands down their trouser legs. A car hooted and I stepped back as it swung into the narrow entry, drenching me in light. It swished past and, following its bouncing tail-light with dazzled eyes I saw no cart, and no men.

I got home at twenty-five past nine and the door was locked, so I knew Dad had gone out. I'd have been glad, except that after what I'd seen in the alley I could have fancied a bit of company. Anyway I let myself in and found he hadn't even cleared the table. Our plates and cutlery were where we'd left them, crusted now with congealed yellow sauce. I hung my anorak up and headed for the sink and then I changed my mind and left it.

When I came down next morning he was sitting in the middle of all this squalor, drinking coffee and reading the paper. Without looking up he said, "This place is a bit of a tip isn't it, Lucy?"

"Sure is," I replied brightly.

"You didn't do the washing up."

"Neither did you. Is there any toast?"

"There's bread, Lucy, and a toaster. I hope you're not planning to leave it like this indefinitely?"

"How are you planning to leave it, Dad?"

He sighed. "You've obviously been listening to your mother's friends, young woman. Have you any idea how hard I have to work to keep this very expensive roof over your head and keep you in the manner to which you have always been accustomed?"

"I have an idea, Dad, yes. But I work hard too. At school. I think we should share the housework till Mum comes home."

"Oh, you do, do you?" He folded the paper brusquely, so that it rattled, and threw it on the table. "The trouble with you, Lucy, is that you take everything for granted. No gratitude. Oh, and by the way. You'll have to get the bus this morning. I'm not going in. Things to see to here."

Like I said, there was something on his mind, and it turned out to be a pretty sneaky something too, in my opinion.

Twenty-Three

THE POISON CLOUD WAS ONLY fifteen miles from Paris when the wind changed. The papers had been running a sort of countdown to disaster, and now they ran big black headlines about a miracle, as though all of the French lived in Paris and everything was okay. There'd been nothing more in the local rag about Mum and Mabel and the others deciding to camp in Pitfield Lane. In fact, once the miracle story had been milked dry, the press seemed to lose interest in matters nuclear, and I was surprised when I got a message to go and see Mrs. Kelsey. She's in charge of girls' welfare, so I knew what it'd be about and I wondered how the school had found out. I still don't know. Anyway, I went along to see her at morning break.

"Hello Lucy."

"'Lo, Miss."

"Sit down. D'you know why I've sent for you?"

"I think so, Miss. Is it about my mum?"

"That's right. She isn't with you at present, is she?"

"No, Miss. She's living under some bin-liners in Pitfield Lane."

"Quite. And how do you feel about that, Lucy? Are you coping without her – you and your father? Is there an aunt or somebody who could pop in to cook and so forth?"

"No aunt, Miss. They're all down south. We manage, Miss."

"Good. Not feeling unduly upset then – eating properly – managing homework and so on?"

"Yes, Miss."

"Splendid. Well." She smiled and stood up. "I expect your mother will be back with you before long, Lucy, and in the meantime if there are any problems – anything you'd like to talk to me about – you know I'm always here."

"Yes, Miss."

Maudlyn laughed when I told her what I'd said about bin-liners. "Kelsey didn't laugh, though," I told her. "Didn't even smile. She just said "Quite", and carried on as though I'd said Mum had popped down the shop for a packet of shredded wheat."

"Told you, didn't I? I said you were fussing too much over what your folks do. She'll have heard far weirder stories than yours, Lucy – you can bet on it." Old Maudlyn. She should be available on the National Health.

The rest of the day was uneventful, as they say. Tim's father mustn't have been working late because Tim wasn't at the bus stop, so I didn't have to tell him I hadn't asked about the party yet. I'd been expecting him to grab me about it at school, but he must've forgotten or something.

When I got home the place was tidy and Dad was burning leaves in the garden. He'd been to the village and bought sausages and I cooked them and we had sausages and green beans and baked potatoes. Afterwards I washed and he wiped and I thought everything might turn out okay after all, only there was something peculiar about his manner. I couldn't put my finger on it but he seemed uneasy, as though he was waiting for something to happen. When we'd finished clearing up he went off to his study and I played records in my room till bedtime.

I'd been asleep for a while when I was woken by a loud noise. The wind had risen, it was raining heavily and somebody was banging on the front door. I sat up and looked at the clock radio on my bedside unit. Twenty past eleven. Dad seldom goes to bed before midnight and I listened for his footsteps in the hallway. Whoever was knocking kept right on knocking and it sounded pretty urgent, but there was no response from Dad. Maybe he'd gone to bed early. He's a pretty heavy sleeper. You could go twelve rounds with a wild pig right in his bedroom and he wouldn't even stir, so I decided I'd better go down myself. I got out of bed and wrapped myself in my dressing-gown and went out on to the landing. I was shivering, and only partly from the cold. I had this picture of myself opening the door to find two men with a handcart on the step. I was surprised to see that there was a light on somewhere below, and when I got to the top of the stairs and looked down, Dad was standing in the hallway, watching the door.

"Dad?" He glanced up and I hissed "Who is it?" I was scared. It must be burglars or murderers or something, or else why would he stand there instead of answering the door?

"Go back to bed, Lucy."

"But who is it?"

Before he could answer me, I heard Mum's voice. "Phillip?"

Dad didn't reply, and I shouted "Dad – it's Mum. Open the door."

"Go back to bed!"

"No. What's happening?" I came halfway down the stairs and called "Mum?"

"Lucy – what's the matter with this door – I can't get in."

It was then I realised what he'd done – why he'd stayed home today and why he'd seemed uneasy. I turned on him. "You've changed the locks, haven't you?"

"Yes, I have. And now I want you to go back to bed, Lucy, because this matter is between me and your mother. Go along."

"No! You can't lock Mum out. It's raining. She might be ill or in danger. I'm going to open the door." I was crying. I ran down the stairs but he'd stationed himself between me and the door and was standing with his arms spread wide to block my passage.

I swung round the newel-post and ran back toward the kitchen. He called sharply and I heard him coming after me.

There was a new lock on the side door, too, with a shiny key in it. I twisted the key and jerked the door open. Rain hit my face, and I was pelting along the side of the house in my bare feet, my dressing-gown flapping in the wind.

"Lucy!" Dad was close behind. Mum had abandoned her attempt to get in and had left the garden. I could see the gleaming top of Mabel's Suzuki beyond the hedge. As I ran down the path, its engine started. I tore through the gateway and across the pavement, grabbing the handle of the passenger door. It was locked. I battered on the window and saw Mum's startled face through the rain-beaded glass. She leaned across and flipped the lever and I wrenched the door open, scrambling up into the high seat. Dad was in the gateway. I slammed the door and locked it. Instead of pulling away, Mum sat and looked at me with an exasperated expression on her face.

"What d'you think you're doing, Lucy? Look at you – barefoot and soaked to the skin. Go back to the house at once and change."

"No!" Dad was peering in, slapping the glass with his palm, mouthing. I gripped the edge of the seat with both hands and looked straight ahead. "I'm not going back. Never. He changed the locks. Drive away, Mum, please!"

"I can't take you with me, Lucy – you'd catch your death of pneumonia. There's nothing for you to wear."

"I don't care Mum. You're stuck with me so you might as well drive on."

She did so, with an impatient noise and a toss of the head. Dad strode alongside while the Suzuki was gathering speed but I refused to look at him.

The rest's a bit of a blur. Mum never said a word as we swished up the shiny road. I could tell she was mad by the jerky way she drove, and I knew her anger was directed more at me than at Dad, too. I sat there, shivering and smouldering at the same time. Well – I

83

wasn't the one who'd shut her out, was I? Anybody'd think she didn't want me.

It was pitch dark in Pitfield Lane. Mum drove onto the verge and switched off, and Mabel and someone called Jan came and exclaimed over me, and Jan fetched a thick tartan travel rug to wrap me in. Some other women were bobbing about in the torchlight and Mum said she hadn't managed to get her kagoul because Phillip had changed the locks. Somebody said typical, and they started saying things about men which I was too shattered and upset to take in.

They put me in the back of the vehicle, where there were sleeping bags and blankets and stuff and I soon got warm between Mum and this Jan character, who were using the Suzuki as a bedroom. I heard rain on the roof for a while, and then I fell asleep.

Twenty-Four

WE WERE UP AT SIX AND IT WAS COLD. Really cold. There was mist between the trees and a heavy dew on the grass that looked like frost. There were six women, not counting me. Mum, Mabel, Jan, Cathy, Midge and Kerry. Tom had refused to have anything to do with camping full time. Apparently he and Mabel had had a terrific row about it. Two by two, we went along the lane to Alice's for a pee, a wash and a spot of brekky. Alice was one of those old folks who get up at about five a.m. even though they've nowhere to go and she was a godsend to us. Day after day, as our protest continued, she would be ready at six with a fire, a pot of tea and a big plateful of toast, and each pair would thaw out in front of the fire for ten minutes or so while they ate and drank. There were seven with me, of course, and that first morning I went with Kerry and Mabel. Kerry was a student at the university. She went off to lectures two days a week but came back and slept at the camp. In her spare time she played saxophone in a band.

I'd no clothes with me except my nightie and dressing gown. The women had rummaged in the bin-liners they used for wardrobes and kitted me out as best they could, but I must have looked some kind of a sight when I walked in Alice's door. She didn't bat an eye. "Hello, love," she said. "The bathroom's through there and you don't take sugar, do you?"

There was no bathroom, of course – just a privy in the back yard and a shallow sink to wash in, but it was lovely sitting right up close to that fire taking gulps of scalding tea and munching toast.

When we got back Mum said, "What about school, Lucy?" I spread my arms and looked down at myself. "I can't go like this, Mum, can I? Maybe tonight I could call in home and get some of my stuff so I can go tomorrow."

"If your father will let you in," she said. She's very dry, my mum.

Thinking about how I looked reminded me that Tim would be passing in an hour or so with his dad. It seems daft now, but at the time I was more bothered about that than anything else. I couldn't stand the thought of him seeing me dressed up like Worzel Gummidge in Mabel's wellies and Kerry's beat-up hat. I lurked about, listening for the Range Rover's engine, and when I heard it I went in the trees behind the bender till they'd gone. I pretended I was getting sticks for the fire because I was afraid Midge and Kerry might laugh at me. They don't believe in dressing to please men.

Anyway, just after that we heard another engine and it was Dad. We were sitting round the fire, all except

Cathy, who was down by the main road on lookout. He pulled up nearby and stuck his head out.

"I've come to take you home, Lucy."

I shook my head. "I want to stay here, Dad."

"What about school?"

"She's taking the day off today," Mum told him. "After last night's trauma."

"It's against the law to keep a child from school, Margaret."

"It's against ordinary decency to lock one's wife out of her home, Phillip." She injected a lot of poison into that rendition of my dad's first name.

"I can't go in these clothes, anyway," I said.

"I'll fetch your clothes if you insist on remaining here." He looked at Mum. "And I shall be looking into what the law says about enticing minors away from their homes."

"Don't be absurd, Phillip. She's here from choice and she's with her mother. I think you'll find it's all within the law."

He turned round and drove off, but twenty minutes later the car reappeared at the end of the lane and he left a suitcase full of my stuff with Cathy. Changing into my own clothes I felt a bit sorry for him. I'd tried not to take sides and I hadn't. Not really. I mean, just because I'd been living at home with him didn't mean I was against Mum, and I wasn't against him now that I was here with her. It was changing the locks that did it. The shock.

Anyway, here I was, living like a dosser with winter coming on and it's funny, but I bet I felt as lonely sitting by the fire with Mum and Jan and the others as he did all alone in his big, daft house.

Twenty-Five

WE HAD BEANS AND COFFEE FOR LUNCH, heated over the fire. It only needed John Wayne to come loping in but instead we got Sefton Pratt. He's the guy Mabel and Tom overheard in the Fleece. He tied his B.M.W. to the old hitching post and came over.

"Good afternoon, ladies." Smile when you say that, I thought.

"What d'you want?" growled Mabel, who remembered him.

"To talk," he said. "May I sit down?"

"Suit yourself. Sit here if you want." Mabel vacated the upturned bucket she'd been sitting on, stacked our plates and mugs and carried them off to Alice's. Pratt gazed after her for a moment, then sat down on the bucket and rubbed his hands together. "I'm Pratt. Sefton Pratt. Chilly, isn't it?"

"We know who you are," said Mum, "and we've

noticed the cold, too. Especially at night. So the sooner you and that precious company of yours leave Apton Magna the better."

"That's what I want to talk to you about."

"Oh yes – pulling out, are you?"

Pratt shook his head. "'Fraid not. Look." He leaned forward with a very sincere expression on his face. "My company understands your concern, but it's based on a misconception. You see, there's more than one way of burying nuclear waste. The place they bombed in France was a shallow burial site. Pit Field will be a deep site, completely invulnerable to any sort of penetration. There's absolutely no danger."

"You're bound to say that, though, aren't you?" challenged Cathy. "I mean, I don't suppose the people who made that dump in France said to the locals, 'This is a highly vulnerable installation we're shoving on to you folks. One little bomb and — pouf!'"

"Yes," said Midge. "How do we know you're telling the truth? How come you don't put these places near your own homes if they're so safe? How far's the closest one to your house, Mr. Pratt?"

"Oh, let me see now." He did a rapid calculation in his head. "Eighty, eighty-five miles. That's approximate."

"Right. And that's approximately how far we want to be from one, too – if we can't get rid of nuclear power altogether."

Pratt's smile had a rueful twist to it. "Get rid of nuclear power – the six of you?"

"Seven," Mum corrected. "There's Kerry, watching the road."

"Eight if you count Alice," I put in, and Jan nodded.

"We mustn't forget Alice, just because she's not actually camping."

Pratt nodded. "Eight, then, out of a population of what – two, two and a half thousand? Hardly a majority."

"Majorities aren't always right," said Jan. "In the thirties, the majority of Germans supported Hitler, and we all know they weren't right, don't we?"

"You can't win, you know. Winter's coming, and you've no facilities here. You might as well pack up and go home."

"We've got facilities," I said, "At Alice's."

"Ah, but your friend Alice won't be here much longer, love."

"How d'you mean?"

Before he could answer, Mabel called to us. She was coming along the lane in a hurry. "Kick him out!" she shouted, pointing at Pratt. "You wait till you know what he's done – you won't want to talk to him then."

Pratt got up. "Your friend seems a bit steamed up," he said. "I think perhaps I'd best be off." He walked over to his car, trying not to look as though he was hurrying, but you could tell he wanted to be in it before Mabel arrived. Seeing him cross the track she put on a spurt, and he only just got the door shut in time. She bent and yelled at him through the windscreen as he started up. You couldn't tell if his face was red because of the tinted glass but I bet it was. The tyres screeched, and Mabel jumped back as the car shot away in reverse. We all stood and stared after him as he swung out on to the main road and roared off. Then we looked at Mabel.

"What's happened?" asked Mum.

"It's Alice. They're taking her cottage. She has to move out within three weeks and she's dreadfully upset. I think one of us ought to go and sit with her."

I wanted to go but they wouldn't let me. Said I wasn't old enough. We were all going to end up there in the middle of the night anyway, but we didn't know that then.

Twenty-Six

MABEL STAYED WITH ALICE. The rest of us worked around the camp, gathering wood, looking after the fire and making soup for the evening meal. The Ogdens drove by while I was peeling onions. I didn't know the vehicle was there till it had gone past and I gazed after it, wondering if Tim had spotted me.

By the time we'd eaten and washed up it was dark, and we sat round the fire, talking and singing. It was cold, and we must have been a weird-looking bunch, padded out in as many layers of tatty gear as we could get on. If you can imagine fat scarecrows, you've got it. We sang, but to tell you the truth we were feeling pretty low. We were thinking about what they were doing to Alice and asking ourselves what chance you have when people can kick you out of the house you've lived in all your life. "Do you still believe we can win?" murmured Cathy at one point, looking at Mum. Mum nodded. "I do, and so must you. So must we all. If we stop believing in ourselves, we're finished."

Around nine, Mum looked at her watch. "Bedtime, Lucy."

"Aw, Mum—"

"Never mind aw Mum. School tomorrow."

"I know, but can't I just—"

"No."

Everybody said goodnight, and I went over and got in the back of the Suzuki. I don't suppose you've ever got ready for bed in the back of a Suzuki so I'll tell you, it's not easy. The temptation is to sleep in your clothes but if you do you soon start to smell, so you twist about, banging your knuckles and elbows on bits of sharp metal as you wriggle out of your gear. The stuff you're taking off is warm and dry, but the things you put on will be damp and cold because everything gets like that when you're dossing, and you know that by morning the things you're taking off will be like that too, and sometimes beetles get into them and run down you when you put them on. You want to try it sometime. It's brilliant.

Anyway I flicked a slug off my sleeping bag and got in and lay listening to the murmur of the women's voices and the wind in the trees. I thought about Alice, and Maudlyn, and Tim, and what Dad was doing, and this and that and one thing and another, and I couldn't sleep. The wind was rising, and presently I heard the spat of raindrops hitting the roof and the women exclaiming as they got up and made a dash for shelter. When Mum and Jan got in the car I pretended I was asleep and not long after that I was.

I woke up with the wind roaring and rain drumming

93

and somebody screaming. Jan and Mum were heaving about, cursing as they tried to locate their shoes in the cramped, pitch-black space.

"What's wrong, Mum – who's that screaming?" I sat up and pressed my forehead to the cold glass, trying to see out.

"I don't know, Lucy. Stay here. Maybe the wind's taken the bender."

They opened the door and piled out and the wind slammed in, flinging sharp rain in my face. I gasped, and began groping for my clothes. The screaming had stopped, but I heard shouts, and some of the voices were men's. I'd pulled on my jeans and was trying to find my shoes when I saw a large, pale hand flatten itself on the window not six inches from my cheek. Dim figures were jostling outside. Somebody laughed, and then the Suzuki began to rock. I cried out, feeling for something to hold onto – grabbing at empty air. The rocking grew more violent and I was sliding and rolling this way and that among an invisible jumble of bedding, clothes and equipment. I heard the roar of an engine, and the inside of the Suzuki was illuminated briefly by the headlights of a passing vehicle. Somebody shouted. The rocking stopped. The door, which I'd slammed against the rain, was flung open. Hands reached in. I tried to crawl out of reach, right up against the backs of the seats, but a hand closed round my ankle and I was hauled out, catching my cheek on some sharp object and falling heavily into the mud.

Figures were bending over me, laughing. Hands plucked and pummelled. Fingers poked and prodded. I rolled under the vehicle and lay with my teeth bared and the back of my head against a wheel, lashing out with naked feet at the leering faces of those who knelt in the mud, reaching for me.

I don't suppose I'd have kept them off for long, but two more vehicles swept by and somebody shouted, "Okay lads, that's it," and they got up and ran off into the dark.

I stayed right where I was, though, sodden and shivering, till I heard Mum calling me. I tried to answer, but only managed a croak. I crawled out from under the Suzuki on limbs that shook so much they barely supported me, and when Mum found me I threw my arms round her neck and cried like I'd never stop.

The bender had gone, and our stuff was scattered in the trees. Jan decided we couldn't do anything in the dark so we set off for Alice's. Halfway we met Mabel, who'd seen vehicles turning on to Pit Field and had set off to see what was happening.

We flopped on Alice's floor and the old woman fussed about in her nightie, making us tea as though she'd no troubles of her own. I was still shaking and Midge and Kerry were crying quietly with their arms round each other. After a bit, Jan came and put her arms round me and it was like when Maudlyn held me. In a little while the shivering stopped and then I must have fallen asleep, because the next thing I knew it was daylight and I was lying on Alice's beat-up sofa.

Twenty-Seven

Mum noticed I was awake and came over. "All right, lovey?"

"Yes, I think so. Where is everybody?" Cathy and Alice were doing dishes. There was nobody else in the room.

"Jan, Midge and Kerry have gone to look at the damage and try to set up camp again, and Mabel's gone to phone the press about last night."

"What was it, Mum? Who were they?"

"We don't know, Lucy. Mabel thinks they were local hooligans who'd been paid by NERDS to keep us busy while they got their vehicles on to Pit Field. They've done that, by the way. There's a truck with what looks like drilling equipment, and some sort of caravan. I'm not sure, though – I can't believe even NERDS would stoop to using thugs against us."

I sat up. Cathy said "Coffee, love?" I nodded. My mouth was dry and I had a stiff jaw. I felt my cheek.

"Is there a bruise?"

Mum nodded. "The papers should print your picture – show what's happening to peaceful protest nowadays. Does it hurt very badly, darling?"

"No. Is everybody else all right?"

She nodded again. "Luckily, their leader, if that's what he was, called 'em off as soon as the vehicles had passed. God knows what might have happened otherwise."

Cathy came across with a steaming mug. "Here, love – you'll feel better with some of this inside you. How's the face?"

"Okay, thanks." I nodded towards the old woman, working at the sink with her back to us, and whispered, "How's Alice – over the shock a bit, is she?"

Cathy shrugged and pulled a face. "I think she's in a daze, Lucy – says she won't be here in three weeks, anyway. You don't really get over things, you know – not at that age."

I sat on the sofa, sipping my coffee and watching Alice. She was working away as always, but her movements were sort of mechanical and slow. She was less birdlike, if you know what I mean.

It was half past seven when I finished my coffee. Nobody had mentioned school, and I'd begun to hope Mum had forgotten, but she hadn't. At twenty to eight Midge came in with a great bundle of clothes and shoes and stuff she'd rescued from the wreck of the camp, and she brought my shoes and uniform, too. Typical adult. It wasn't wet or muddy like the other stuff, either, because it had been in the Suzuki, so there was no excuse. I put it on slowly, wishing I'd made a big thing out of my sore cheek.

Midge was going back to the camp so I walked down with her. The rain had stopped, but there were massive puddles in the lane and a cold wind blew rags of cloud across a pale blue sky. On Pit Field, a man was walking about with his head down and his hands in his pockets, kicking stones, while five or six others stood watching him. We gazed across at them as we passed, but none of them looked at us.

"What's the point of us staying here," I asked, "now that they're on the field?"

Midge shook her head. "This doesn't really change anything, Lucy. We never believed we could stop NERDS getting on to Pit Field. They'd have used the courts against us as soon as they saw we weren't going to be bought off by Sefton Pratt and his community centre. Our camp's a statement — it says that some of us do not give our consent to what's happening, and that's important. We attract publicity, which stirs people's conscience and forces them to think about the issues, whereas NERDS and the council and the government would prefer them to concentrate on East Enders and Princess Di while they get on with doing what they want to do."

By the time we reached the camp site Jan and Kerry had rigged up a new bender, using a massive sheet of polythene Alice had given us. It was off a mattress she'd bought years ago and she'd hung on to it, thinking it might come in useful. That's what she told Jan, but I wouldn't be surprised if she'd had one of her dreams and knew it would be needed someday.

Anyway, there it was, on its frame of sycamore saplings, and if anything it was better than the old one. The two women were busy searching the wet undergrowth for bits of equipment which our attackers had thrown about. Pans, mugs, spoons and wellies lay in a pile on the verge, and articles of sodden clothing had been draped over shrubs to dry. I wished I could stay and help, but I knew there was no point suggesting it. When it comes to the crunch, adults stick together.

I said, "See you," and dawdled on down the lane to the road. I crossed and walked the few yards to the bus-stop. It was the stop Tim used when he travelled by bus and so of course I started thinking about him, and I made up this fantasy.

It's three, four weeks from now. Alice has gone. Her cottage is boarded up. It's late evening, around half-nine. Mum and the other women have been arrested and taken to Bradford. I've avoided arrest by hiding in the woods, and am in sole charge of the camp. It's a wet, windy night, the Suzuki's been towed away, and I'm just getting ready to kip down in the bender when this forlorn figure comes lurching along the lane. It's Tim, in his stocking feet and shirt-sleeves. "Lucy," he croaks, falling into my arms, half-dead with cold, "my father has learned of my love for you and has cast me out. I have no relatives, save a maiden aunt in John o' Groats, and I'm cold – so cold. Permit me to stay with you here in this bender, and together we'll defy the world."

Brilliant, right? Except that three seconds later he went roaring past with his dad in the Range Rover and didn't even look at me, though he must have seen me standing there.

I didn't go in by bus though, because a couple of minutes later Dad picked me up. I didn't know whether I wanted to get in the car or not and I stood there trying to decide, and he said, "Come on, Lucy, for goodness' sake – people will think I'm a child snatcher or something." I got in.

He asked me to come home and I said not till Mum does. Then he asked how I was managing and I told him about the raid and he got really worried and said the whole thing was ridiculous and it was time to call it quits and come home. I said he knew Mum wouldn't, and repeated that I wouldn't till she did, and then he started on about slaving to give me a nice home and me preferring the back of a Japanese truck. I sat there wishing I'd waited for the bus.

Maudlyn was hanging round the gateway, looking for me. "Wow, do you look rough!" she said, cheerfully. "Is it right you're in camp with your mum now?"

I nodded. "How did you find out?"

She shrugged. "Grapevine. Everybody knows."

It turned out Dad had called in school yesterday to have a word with Mrs. Kelsey, and it'd got out like things do. I had to go see Kelsey at break, and she looked at my crumpled uniform and muddy shoes and said she doubted I could be getting enough sleep and how did I propose to cope with homework. I told her about Alice and said I guessed I could do my homework at her place. I didn't mention they were chucking her out.

Kelsey had just let me go when I ran into my old pal Amanda in the yard. Amanda Lawrence. She was with Tamsin Murgatroyd. She said, "Hey Tam – look at the state of those shoes."

"Listen, Lawrence," I said. She didn't scare me anymore. I don't know why. "I can always clean my shoes, but your face is gonna stay like it is whatever you do."

That wasn't the best bit, though. Remember Airey, the history guy? Well, we were doing the thirties with him, the rise of Hitler, and he was saying how most Germans were dead enthusiastic over Hitler at the time, and they weren't really bothered about what his followers were doing to the Jews and that, but there was a small resistance movement. "A tiny group of brave individuals," Airey called them, "who dared to swim against the tide, and whom we now know to have been absolutely right, though they were scorned and hated at the time."

I shot my hand up. "You mean like AMANDA, sir? We're scorned and hated, sir, but maybe people will see we were right someday."

You should have seen his face. He stood there for a bit, gob-smacked as they say in this part of the world, and then he went, "Ah – well — not exactly – I mean, I don't think you can compare . . . " Some of the kids were sniggering and his voice tailed off. I fixed him with what I hoped was a keen, enquiring expression until finally he mumbled, "Well, yes – I suppose that's an illustration – an imperfect illustration, of the sort of thing. . . ." He dropped his eyes and it was like all the humiliation he'd inflicted on me cancelling out. It was magic.

Twenty-Eight

"Brrr!" Alice shivered as she let me in. "There's a right old nip in the air tonight, love. I don't know how you stand it down at that camp."

"We cuddle up," I told her.

"Well, rather you than me, all the same. Is it the lav you're wanting, or d'you fancy a cup of tea?"

I shook my head. "Neither, thanks. I just came to see you."

"That's nice." She closed the door and shoved this draught excluder up against it with her foot. It was an old stocking stuffed with rags which looked like a giant pink sausage. "Sit yourself by the fire then, and I'll put the kettle on."

We drank tea and gossiped a bit – the weather, school, what the men were doing on the field and all that. After a bit I said, "It's funny, but I feel a lot better since I left home. It's like I was stuck in the middle before, but now I've made my mind up and I know I'm doing the right thing and it's not complicated anymore and I don't even notice the cold."

Alice nodded. "It's good to believe in something, Lucy — to know who you are." I nodded and smiled and said yes because that was it exactly. I knew who I was, only I wouldn't have known how to put it into words like that.

"It's good to believe in something," she went on. "But you mustn't let it become the only thing in your life. There are so many things in the world, Lucy. Things to see. Things to do. Experiences. Other people. Other points of view. Don't make the mistake I made, or you'll end up dying without ever having really lived."

I nodded, watching pictures changing in the fire. I didn't know what she was on about really but it was nice sitting in that warm, shadowy room with Alice, talking. If I'd known it was the last time I'd have told her I loved her, but I didn't, and now it's too late. She knew things, though, and I expect she knew that, too. At least I hope she did.

Twenty-Nine

NOTHING MUCH HAPPENED in the next few days. Saturday night I met Maudlyn in town and we had a few coffees and some laughs. Monday Tim came up to me in the yard and asked about the party and I told him I'd asked Mum and she'd said yes. I don't know why I said that – I suppose I was just fed up having it hanging over me. I think I knew I wasn't going to mention it to Mum, anyway. It didn't seem appropriate somehow, living the way we were. I can't explain, but I'd sort of decided when the time came I'd slip off up the track as though I was off to Alice's, and hope nobody'd notice I'd taken special care over my appearance.

Every morning a truckload of workers arrived to join the handful living in the caravan on Pit Field, and they'd spend the day shoving earth around and drinking mugs of tea before bouncing past us again at half past five. Sometimes there'd be a police car with them but we never tried to stop them. We'd wave our placards and they'd call out dirty comments and then we'd traipse through the blue exhaust, back to our chores. The attack on our camp was supposed to be under investigation but it got no further. Lovely Lawrence and her sidekicks made snide comments on my appearance and I retaliated, taunting Lawrence about her looks and Murgatroyd about her ludicrous name. Tamsin Murgatroyd. Tamsin pillocking Murgatroyd. I wondered how the vicar managed to keep a straight face at her christening.

The thirty-first was my birthday. It was a Saturday. In the morning Mabel took me with her to Bradford in the Suzuki to buy grub and nobody mentioned my birthday. Not even Mum. I thought everybody'd forgotten, but when we got back they'd got this surprise party ready for me. There was all sorts of fancy food laid out on a blanket, and parcels, and a cake baked by Alice. Alice came down to see me cut it, and they all sang Happy Birthday, and I opened the parcels and there was a scarf and mittens and leg-warmers and a cap – somebody must've been knitting like mad for days while I was in school – and some gorgeous shoes from Mum and Vulcan Pan's latest album from Dad. There were two cards – one from Maudlyn, addressed to me at The Women's Camp, Pitfield Lane, Apton Magna, which got a cheer from everybody, and one which Cathy'd made out of leaves and flowers and everybody had signed. I cried, partly because Dad wasn't there and had sent this sad, inappropriate gift I couldn't even play; and partly because everybody'd taken the trouble to plan all this in secret for me when they were cold and uncomfortable, and when there were so many more important things to occupy their hands and minds.

I cried, but I was happy. Really happy. We sat round the fire and linked arms and sang, and the love that flowed through our unbroken circle was the greatest force there is.

Thirty

AND SO IT ROLLED ROUND. Wednesday November fourth. When I'd been invited to the party my excitement had been intense. November fourth had seemed a billion years away and I'd constructed fantasies around the event to pass the time. Now that it was here, I was disappointed to find that most of my excitement had evaporated, so that if Tim had asked me for the first time today I'd probably have said no.

Don't get me wrong. I was still mad keen on him. It wasn't that. I suppose it had something to do with the way my life had changed since he invited me. I knew who I was, and I also knew who I wasn't, and I wasn't the sort of person who wants to go to a party where she doesn't know most of the people who'll be there – a party being thrown on the sly in a house whose owner is away. If you must know, I was nervous. I worried about it all day at school. I mentioned it to Maudlyn at break and she said, "Don't go. I wouldn't. We could meet up for a few cokes instead."

She'd almost persuaded me, or maybe I'd almost persuaded myself, when Tim caught up with me on the corridor at hometime. "Hi, Lucy," he grinned. "All set for tonight, then?"

"Oh sure, yes." I couldn't say no to him, you see, and besides he'd taken me by surprise. Anyway, that was it. I'd promised. On the bus I remembered what Alice had said about not letting your cause become the only thing in your life. Well, I wasn't, was I? I was off to a party. It'd be all right.

It started drizzling at five so we ate our meal in the Suzuki. I must have been quieter than usual because Midge said, "What's up, Lucy – bad day at school?"

I shook my head. "No. I was just thinking."

Mum peered at me. "Not ill, are you, dear?"

"No, I'm fine, really." I felt a stab of irritation, and filled my mouth with stew to show I didn't want to talk. Living right up close with people is great a lot of the time – the sharing and the singing and all that. You get really close, but it can get on your nerves as well. You can't go anywhere or do anything without somebody knowing about it. People are watching all the time, and they know you so well it's like they even know what you're thinking. There are no secrets. I think everybody needs their own space where they can get away from people – even the people they love.

There wasn't a lot I could do about my appearance. I always changed out of uniform when I got back from school so I could do my chores without worrying about the mud, which was everywhere and getting worse, with trucks going backwards and forwards and winter coming on. I usually wore jeans and a sweater in the evening, but these were all crumpled and plastered with mud and I certainly couldn't go to a party like that.

I had one dress, but even that was grubby because I'd had to wear it once or twice while my jeans were being washed. I thought of calling home and fetching another dress or at least some clean jeans, but I couldn't think of a good enough excuse without mentioning the party, and it was too late for that. So this one would have to do. Even then, I'd be lucky if nobody wanted to know why I was wearing a dress when my jeans were available. Oh, boy.

To get around this problem I let my jeans fall out the back of the Suzuki. As they landed in the slimy puddle I gave a yell so everybody was looking when I fished them out. What a mess!

I did my jobs, taking care not to get fresh mud on my dress. When I'd finished I brushed my greasy hair and put on the shoes Mum gave me for my birthday. When I'd done the best I could, I looked in the mirror. It was about four inches across and didn't show much, but I saw enough to know I looked like somebody who lives in the bottom half of a dustbin. I tucked a couple of books under my arm and set off, calling, "Mum – I'm off up to Alice's to do homework. I won't be late." I thought I'd just call in on the party – have the odd coke and dance for a bit, then leave. That way I'd have kept my promise, and been close to the gorgeous Tim for a while.

Halfway up the track I had the idea of leaving the books at Alice's. I could say I was calling at Tim's without mentioning any party, or that his dad was away.

It had stopped raining but it was very dark, and I had

to take care not to step in any of the deep, water-filled ruts the trucks had made. Presently I came opposite to Pit Field and glanced across. In the feeble light from the caravan window I saw that two of the men were still working – lifting things off a wheelbarrow and letting them fall into a hole in the ground. I was about to give them the old two-finger salute when I realised it wasn't a wheelbarrow at all but a handcart. *The* handcart. I recoiled, biting my bottom lip to keep from crying out, and pounded on Alice's door.

She knew exactly where I was going. I ought to have expected that, of course. "You're early, Princess," she said. "You'll be the first to arrive at the ball." Then she peered into my face and said "Why – whatever's the matter, love – you look as though you've seen a ghost."

I didn't know if she was joking. It was hard to tell with Alice. I jerked my head in the direction of Pit Field. "I've just seen those two guys with the handcart. I swear they're following me around."

"No, Lucy," she said. "They are not. You are no more real to them than they are to you. Come in a minute – it's no fun being early for a party, and not a good idea either – he'll be thinking you're eager."

I glanced over my shoulder as I stepped inside. "They're pretty real to me," I said. I showed her the books. "I want to leave these."

She closed the door and eyed me sternly. "I ought not to be encouraging you, you know – deceiving your mother. Going to a party where there'll be no adult to keep an eye on you. I ought to take you back."

I looked at her. "Didn't you ever sneak off when you were a girl, Alice?"

"Never, Lucy. I wish now that I had, but, you see, I was the dutiful daughter so here I stayed, and gradually this place became the whole of my world — so that eventually I didn't even want to go anywhere, anymore. And besides." She smiled ruefully. "I was ugly, and there weren't many invitations for ugly girls in those days."

"You're not ugly."

"Yes, I am. Look." She turned her head so I saw it in profile. "Don't you think I look rather like a falcon?"

Jesus! She'd landed on the exact comparison I'd made myself, the first time I saw her. My face went hot and I didn't know where to put myself. She laughed, took the books from me and nodded towards the window. "See — there's a car coming. You won't be first now."

I hurried, looking back all the time till I was clear of Pit Field. Nothing followed. I teetered up the last bit of track, trying to keep from splashing my shoes and hoping it wouldn't peter out into a messy farmyard. It didn't, because the place had been tarted up. A pair of white gates opened on to an expanse of concrete in front of the house. Electrified carriage lamps blazed on either side of the door, illuminating a wheelbarrow with dead flowers in it and a millstone propped against the wall. A plaque on the millstone said: "Manor Farm". The car we'd seen passing was parked to one side. I could hear loud music through the door.

I rang the bell, and was patting my hair when it opened. Tim grinned and stepped aside. "Hi, Lucy. Come in." He had some stunning gear on and looked a different person. Feeling like a tramp I followed him across this posh lobby and into a roomful of decibels and dim light. It was a big room, but there were only two people in it. They were quite old – twenty-four, twenty-five maybe, but dressed young, if you know what I mean. They'd been sort of half-dancing – circling each other with glasses in their hands – but they stopped when we came in.

"Lucy – Val and Kevin."

The woman smiled, said "Hello Lucy," and looked me up and down without making it obvious.

Kevin grinned and nodded, but as Tim crossed the room to get me a drink he followed, and the track on the midi ended in time for me to hear him say "Christ almighty, Timmo – what's she come as?" Tim said something I didn't catch and they both laughed.

It was horrible. I knew that Val knew I'd heard, and I didn't know whether to pretend I hadn't, or tell her I was from the camp as a way of excusing the way I looked. In my confusion and embarrassment I didn't do either. I grinned and stammered and would probably have burst out crying and made a complete idiot of myself if the woman hadn't smiled in a sympathetic way and said, "Take no notice of him, love – he's always been pig-ignorant and I should know." She held out a pack of cigarettes. "Here – try one of these."

I took one. I didn't really want it, but the business of putting it between my lips and bending over her lighter pushed the embarrassing moment into the past and gave me something to do with my hands. It helped me feel less of a kid, too, I suppose.

Tim swished past, thrusting a glass into my hand on his way to the door. He returned a moment later with some new arrivals. I recognised one or two – fifth and sixth formers from school, and when I saw the charming Kevin approaching I gave Val a nod and a smile and drifted across to where they'd stationed themselves. Nobody spoke to me, and I stood forlornly on the fringe of the group, brooding over my disappointment in Tim.

If he'd leapt to my defence when Kevin said what he said I wouldn't have given a damn about the stupid remark, but he hadn't. He'd laughed. And now he was all over the room, being charming and fetching people drinks like somebody about twenty years old and paying no attention to me at all. I'd never felt so wretched in my life. I cursed myself for ever having imagined it might be otherwise, and wished like hell I'd listened to old Maudlyn. I told myself I'd drink this one drink, finish my cigarette and leave.

It was cider in my glass. I'd never had it before but I knew what it was. I'd drunk about half of it and I was starting to feel dizzy. The cigarette might have had something to do with it as well. Anyway I started feeling woozy and I should have stopped drinking but I finished it instead. And then this lad, Dennis I think they called him, appeared out of nowhere and took the empty glass and gave me a full one and started talking to me about some band he was in; and I kept taking sips and smiling and nodding and not having the faintest idea what he was on about because I was getting dizzier and dizzier. He kept passing me this long, lumpy cigarette he was smoking, which I know now what it was but I didn't then, saying here, have a drag, so I did. I forget what he talked about when he got through talking about his band, but it must've been something funny because he started giggling and that started me off and we sort of reeled into a corner and sat down in this forest of legs, giggling, and that's where we were when the cops came in.

Thirty-One

I DIDN'T REALISE what was happening at first. There was some sort of commotion out in the hallway and I assumed it was more of Tim's friends arriving. I wasn't taking much notice by then, anyway, because I'd been following Dennis's instructions and drawing really deeply on his foul rollups, and the combination of dope and cider was wrecking my mind.

Anyway, there was all this commotion, and then Dennis yelled look out, it's a bust, and snatched the rollup from between my lips. You probably won't believe this, but it wasn't till he grabbed that thing and crushed it out in a pot plant that I realised it was a joint. Somebody screamed, and then the room was full of uniforms.

I saw Dennis scuttle behind a sofa and tried to follow him, but a policewoman grabbed my wrist and hauled me to my feet. I could hardly stand and she had to half carry me across the room. Others were being led out, some with their arms up their backs. A scuffle broke out in one corner and somebody must have fallen over the midi because there was a horrible screech and the music stopped.

It was raining again. Cold drizzle prickled my cheeks and forehead as I was hustled across the glistening concrete and into the van. There was this guy in a donkey jacket and wellies standing by the van, waving his arms and yelling something about a sick man and calling an ambulance. The word NERDS was printed in big letters across the back of his jacket. I was too drunk, or high, or both, to really appreciate what was happening to me, otherwise I'd have been a lot more scared. I'm not saying I wasn't scared, but I remember giggling in the back of the van as it bumped along, and I only stopped because it was making me want to go to the toilet.

I won't go on about it. They took us to Bradford and put us in this room. There must have been about thirty of us. Tim was there but I avoided looking at him. I was wishing I'd never set eyes on him if you want to know. Some of the kids were crying – probably thinking what'd happen when the cops called their parents. I didn't see Val or Kevin. Most people just sat with their hands between their knees, staring at the floor. Nobody spoke. A policeman sat near the door, keeping an eye on us. Every time somebody wanted to go to the toilet, they had to wait till a policeman or woman could go with them. I started feeling sick, and by the time somebody was free to escort me I was about ready to throw up. I dashed along the corridor with my hand over my mouth and a policewoman at my heels and puked all over the seat. She was very nice about it but somebody was going to have to clean up after me and I felt humiliated.

Anyway, they started taking us out one by one to be questioned. When it was my turn, I gave my address as The Women's Camp, Pitfield Lane, Apton Magna, like on Maudlyn's card. The policeman looked up from the form he was filling in and said, "Your home address, love, please," and I said the camp was my home. I didn't fancy getting Dad involved, I suppose. He said, "Do your parents live there?"

"My mum does."

"Will she be there now?"

"Yes." He sighed, and wrote it down.

Mum wasn't at the camp, as it happened. She was at the front counter of the police station, waiting for me, and I was allowed to go with her as soon as they'd finished with me. They didn't charge me with anything, but said I might be called as a witness or something. I was just glad to get out.

Mabel was outside in the Suzuki. I started to apologise for the trouble I'd caused, and she said it didn't matter as long as I was all right. We drove through empty, glistening streets and out on the Apton Magna road. It was about one in the morning.

Mum sat silent beside me. I'd sobered up a lot by this time, and after a while I said, "How'd they get you so quick?"

"We were there already," said Mum. "When they drove past the camp, some of us followed. We thought something must be going on at Pit Field or Alice's, but we arrived in time to see the van coming away from the farm. I called at Alice's to get you, and it was only then

117

I found out about this party of yours. Why didn't you tell me, Lucy?"

"I dunno. I kept meaning to, but it never seemed like the right time – d'you know what I mean?"

"I know exactly what you mean, young woman. It never seemed like the right time because you knew I'd have forbidden you to go no matter when you'd mentioned it. I don't know what you can have been thinking about, Lucy – going off to a party where everybody was so much older than you, knowing that Mr. Ogden was away. Didn't you realise what might happen – that they might be smoking dope or getting drunk or worse? You're very lucky not to be up in court, you stupid girl."

Oh, boy! It was like that all the way home. Did I realise it'd be in all the papers? What did I think my father'd say when he found out? And the teachers at school? What chance did I think I'd have of getting a job when I left school if I had a criminal record? Nag, nag, flaming nag. And if you think that was an eventful day, stick around – you ain't seen nothing yet.

Thirty-Two

MUM DECIDED I DIDN'T HAVE TO go to school next day so we could all sleep late, but it didn't work because just after eight a police car came up the lane, waking Cathy who then woke the rest of us.

What the heck's up now, we thought, and Midge and I volunteered to go find out. I had a headache and felt rotten but it was the least I could do after last night.

The car was parked by Pit Field. Two coppers and a bunch of workmen stood looking into a hole. It was about fifty yards away so we couldn't see what was in it. "Maybe they struck oil," said Midge.

"I have to pee," I told her. I wanted to talk to Alice. I left her standing there and went and knocked at Alice's door. Alice opened up and said, "Oh, it's you, Lucy. Are you all right?"

"Not really," I said. "D'you know what happened last night – at the farm?"

She nodded. "Your mother was here. I think she

blames me for letting you go. She thinks we conspired together."

I looked at her. "You said something before, about we'd have to wait and see. Did you know what was going to happen, Alice?"

She shook her head. "No, Lucy, I did not. Not exactly, anyway. There was a sense of foreboding, which I didn't recognise at the time, but nothing specific."

"Why didn't you warn me, Alice?"

She smiled sadly. "Would you have believed me, Lucy? Would anything I said have stopped you going to that party?"

I thought about it, and shook my head. "I suppose not. I had a terrific crush on Tim, you see, and where's the harm in a party?"

Alice shrugged. "There you are, you see. I said that the hard part was getting people to believe, and now you know it's true."

When I came out of the lavatory she'd made me a cup of coffee.

"Thanks," I said. "Midge is outside, watching two policemen watching a hole."

"What?"

"A hole. They're standing there, looking into a hole in the field. Midge reckons they've struck oil."

"Ah." She crossed to the window and stood gazing out, twisting her fingers together anxiously. She was still standing there when I finished my coffee and I said, "Are you all right, Alice?"

"Yes, Lucy. I'm all right. I fancy something's ending for me, that's all. We'll take Midge her coffee now, shall we?"

"What d'you mean, something's ending?"

"Come along."

As we stepped outside a car went by, headed for Manor Farm. Midge was standing where I'd left her. There was no sign of anybody on the field.

"What's happening – where is everybody?"

Midge took the cup and shrugged. "They're in the caravan. They walked round the hole a bit, chuntering and kicking bits of clay, then they went in the caravan and I haven't seen them since." She grinned at the old woman. "How's Alice?"

"I'm fine, Midge, thank you. I've had all your breakfasts ready since six o'clock."

"Oh crikey – I'm sorry, love. We had a lie-in. Until the police went past, that is. Is everything spoilt?"

Instead of answering, Alice pointed. "Look – there's somebody coming out."

The caravan door opened and the policemen appeared. They stood in the doorway, talking to somebody inside. I heard a car coming down from the farm. It was the one which had passed a few minutes earlier. There were two people in it. It stopped and a woman got out and came over.

"Excuse me – d'you happen to know whether anyone's in at the farm, only we've phoned and knocked and we can't get any answer. We're from the *Telegraph*."

Midge shook her head. "Sorry. Bit of bother there last night, wasn't there?" She didn't tell the woman I'd been there. I was glad. I wondered where Tim was.

Alice said, "You'll have summat better than that to put in your paper in a minute," and nodded towards

121

the two policemen who were crossing the field towards us.

The reporter looked at them, then at Alice. "Oh yes – why – what's happening?"

"They'll have found the pit, I reckon."

"Which pit?"

"The pit in Pit Field." Alice smiled. "Everybody knows it's called Pit Field, but nobody knows why, except daft Alice Hazelborne."

We were all waiting for her to go on, but before she could enlighten us the coppers reached the gateway and the reporter called out, "Morning. Liz Grimshaw – *Telegraph*. Can you tell me what's happening here?"

The pair were busy trying to negotiate the rutty yellow mud in the gateway without getting their shoes filthy. When they reached the track, one stood by the verge and began wiping the sides of his shoes on the grass while his companion went towards the car. Liz started her spiel again but the copper cut her off. "You'll have to wait." He nodded towards his colleague. "He's calling in. He'll see if it's all right to tell you."

Liz was about to tackle Alice when her companion came over. "What's going on, Liz?" She shrugged.

"Dunno. They're seeking permission to tell us."

"Can we go on the field?" He had a camera and was obviously raring to go. The policeman shook his head. The tinny quack of a radio sounded from the direction of the police car. The NERDS guys came out of their caravan and stood about with their hands in their pockets, glancing in our direction from time to time. Alice said no more, but stood gazing out across the field. Presently the policeman got out of the car and came over, nodding to his colleague, whose shoes were about as clean as they were going to be for now.

"Right," he said, addressing the reporter. "At seven forty-five this morning we received information to the effect that workmen at this site had uncovered what appeared to be human remains. A vehicle was dispatched immediately, and following a preliminary investigation by uniformed officers, detectives and forensic experts were called in. That's all I'm able to say at the present time."

"Can we talk to the men who found the remains?"

"No."

"Can we get a picture?"

"Don't be stupid."

"Do you suspect foul play?"

"No comment."

The phrase "human remains' had triggered my memory. I turned to Alice. "Last night," I said, "Just before I knocked on your door, I saw somebody in the field. Two men with a—" I'd been about to say wheelbarrow, but her expression told me what I'd really seen and my heart lurched. "Two men with a handcart," I breathed.

Alice nodded. "Yes, Lucy. Half the village was carried to the pit on that cart. More than half. And they're still here. Things don't cease to be, just because we hide them in the earth."

The reporter had turned from the policeman and was listening. "Half the village?" she said.

Alice nodded again. "Aye. Two hundred souls, give or take a few. Thirteen forty-nine. The Black Death."

Liz Grimshaw glanced towards Pit Field. "You mean—"

"Aye. That's where they put 'em. There'd be a marker at first, and documents too, but six hundred years is a long time. Stones crumble. Documents are lost. The name's the only thing that's lasted. That, and the Hazelbornes."

My hand flew to my mouth as my dream broke. The village, abandoned. A bundle of rags with bones inside. My reeling mind was throwing up images faster than I could cope with them. Two men, carrying something out of a cottage. Trundling it, laden, in Pitfield Lane. Dropping things into a hole. Alice, weeks ago, saying, "Some Tuesday, long ago . . ." Hidden, but here forever.

Faintly, as though from far away, I heard the reporter ask Alice if she was sure, and how she knew, and then another image flashed up. Rain in my face, and an excited man in a donkey jacket saying something about a sick man and an ambulance, and I blurted it before I thought. Liz Grimshaw turned.

"What was that you said?"

"That man. Last night. Somebody was ill – very ill – here at Pit Field. The police called an ambulance—"

"Oh my God!" She spun on her heel, yelled to the photographer and ran towards the car. We watched, Alice and I, as the vehicle went bouncing off down the track.

And now it begins.

Says Alice.

Thirty-Three

You know how things get around. The old grapevine. The tom-toms. The bush telegraph. Well, it was five to nine when I opened my big mouth. At half past this disc jockey, Mickey Finn, put out the first plague item on Pennine's half-hourly bulletin. Kerry caught it on her tranny. He didn't say the sick guy had the plague – just that he'd been taken ill near a pit containing the remains of plague victims. The item was repeated at ten, and every half hour after that till some doctor phoned in from the local hospital around one to say the guy had salmonella poisoning from sweet and sour prawns.

It was too late. At ten, the NERDS guys fled the site. At twelve thirty a ten year old kid by the name of Byron Ward from the local primary school was eating lunch at home when the item came through on the radio. He heard it, then sat and listened as his mother and the next door neighbour discussed it. They must have indulged in some highly coloured speculation, because Byron returned to school at one fifteen with a very exciting story to tell his friend, and the two of them had a pretty scary rumour going by the time the kids went in for afternoon lessons.

It might have been okay even then, if the teachers had noticed the whispering, the frightened faces. If they'd gathered the kids together and squashed the rumour. If the nit-nurse hadn't arrived.

Little Mandy Chivers was feeling bad. Really bad. She hated to hear all the nasty stuff boys like to talk about, and Norman Conquest had just told her about something called the Black Death, which makes blood come out of your bottom, and which was about to strike down the entire population of Apton Magna, girls first. She looked at Norman out of her eye-corner. Was he telling the truth? He sometimes did. And she was certainly feeling ill. She was trying to remember whether she'd been feeling okay before Norman told her about the Black Death, when there was a tap on the classroom door and the nurse walked in. Mandy uttered a little moan and slid to the floor.

Mandy was the first, but she wasn't the last. Kids are highly suggestible. Within ten minutes they were keeling over right, left and centre, and the head teacher was forced to call the cottage hospital.

Byron Ward was mortified. He gazed about him at his fallen playmates and, realising he might well be held responsible for the carnage, took advantage of the general confusion and slipped away.

He ran home. His mother and Mrs. Conquest from

next door were drinking coffee. He described the scene at school. The panic. The bodies. The ambulance. The nurse. The two women looked at each other, then Mrs. Conquest hurried off to phone her husband.

Mr. Conquest ran a scrapyard out along the Bradford Road. Oedipus Wrecks. As soon as his wife hung up he leapt in his BMW and headed for school to rescue his heir. The head teacher tried to tell him about the salmonella diagnosis and the well-known phenomenon of mass hysteria, but he wasn't listening. He bundled his son into the car, drove home, picked up his wife and such valuables as she'd been able to cram in two plastic carriers, and left town.

The news of their departure sparked off general panic. In less than an hour, cars were leaving Apton Magna like the start of the Italian Grand Prix, their progress hampered by lines of refugees fleeing the village on foot.

We sat on the verge, the seven of us, watching people and vehicles go by. As they passed the end of Pitfield Lane, pedestrians held handkerchiefs over their mouths and sort of swerved outwards to give the lane as wide a berth as possible. It was fantastic. Of course, we didn't get to know any of the details till afterwards, but Kerry's tranny gave us the gist of it. Pennine kept repeating a message from some health chief in Bradford, telling people there was nothing to fear and appealing to them to return to their homes. Meanwhile the national stations had picked up the story and were presenting it in a fairly sensational way, which probably didn't help.

We went down to the end of the track and tried

talking to people as they passed, telling them the NERDS guy had food poisoning, but they wouldn't listen. In fact they backed off and shouted at us to stay away from them. I've never seen people so scared.

Thirty-Four

IT WAS DARK BEFORE THE MESSAGE finally got through. In the meantime we'd had visits from Dad, who was anxious about our health, and from Tom, who tried to get Mabel away.

Around seven, the traffic passing the lane end became two-way, and by eight nobody was leaving anymore. Over the next few hours, nearly everybody was to come slinking back under cover of darkness, feeling daft.

As the excitement began to die down, we started wondering what effect the day's events might have on our struggle. Mabel didn't think it would make any difference. "They'll sweep it all under the carpet. You'll see. In a few days' time it'll be business as usual on Pit Field."

Cathy disagreed. "They can't, Mabel. The place is a grave. Hallowed ground and all that. At the very least there'll be a delay."

129

Mum nodded. "They can't just plough human remains in, or chuck them on a heap. Arrangements will have to be made."

We were sitting round the fire, but we were cold. If you think there's something cosy about a campfire, forget it. It'll warm your front while your back freezes. I didn't say anything, but I was hoping desperately that what had happened might put a stop to the whole affair so we could all go home. I was fed up trying to keep myself and my clothes decent for school, and struggling to keep up with homework too. The thought of homework reminded me that I was supposed to do some biology over the weekend. It was for old Baverstock, and it had to be handed in Monday.

I stood up.

"I have to go up to Alice's," I said. "My homework book's there."

"Give her our love," said Mum, "and tell her they're all coming home. But don't stay chatting, and don't be slipping off to any parties, either."

"Oh, fun-nee."

I set off along the track. The moon was coming up behind the trees and there'd be a touch of frost by morning. I was wearing leg-warmers over my jeans but my feet were numb from sitting cross-legged and I could see my breath.

It was dark, and very quiet. The leafless trees grew close together and their interlaced branches formed a tunnel which splintered the moonlight and stencilled an intricate web of shadow across the lane. Somewhere an owl hooted, and I quickened my pace.

I'd reached the place where the trees thinned, and could see the gleam of moonlight on the cottage roof, when my eye was drawn to a movement in front and to my right. I stopped. A woman was standing in the rutted gateway of Pit Field, looking across at Alice's house. I followed the direction of her gaze, and felt myself go cold. The door was ajar, and a handcart stood beside it.

As I watched, the door opened and a figure backed, shuffling, into the moonlight. A second figure followed, and together they lifted whatever it was they were carrying on to the cart.

You'll have read stuff about people seeing ghosts – how their hackles rise and they're rooted to the spot and all that. It didn't happen with me. Oh, I'm not saying I wasn't scared. I was scared all right, only I wasn't rooted to the spot, and either I don't have hackles, or they stayed right where they were. What blew my mind was knowing that never again would it be possible for me to pretend there's nothing odd about me – I knew I was one of those who see, and I was stuck with it.

They wheeled the cart across the track and through the gateway. The woman followed and I lost sight of them. Thinking about it now, I don't know what it was made me do what I did next. I could have turned and run. I wanted to, but I didn't. What I did was, I moved forward at a sort of half-run till I could see through the gap into the field, and I saw all these people following the cart. Women, men, kids. And then I saw something out of my eye-corner and there was another of them, coming at me down the lane. That's when I finally cracked. I turned to run, twisted my ankle in a rut and fell, and before I could get up its hands were on my arm.

"Lucy – what the heck's up with you, kid?"

It was Tim. I went faint with relief, just like in all the stories, only I didn't throw myself into his arms. I grabbed his sleeve and pointed. "Look!" They were half way across the field and drenched in moonlight.

"What?" he was staring into the gap.

"The people. All those people."

"What people – what're you on about, kid?"

So much for the man who sees.

"Are you all right?" He was staring at me in a scared sort of way.

I nodded. "No thanks to you. You didn't tell me there'd be drugs, did you, or creeps like that Kevin? I'd never have come if I'd known." Boy, was I screwed up about that party. It was guilt, I guess, only I was determined to pin the blame on somebody. I'd had a go at Alice and now it was Tim's turn. He pulled a face.

"I'm sorry, Lucy. I didn't know Kev would be there, honest. He crashed it and he's a pusher. Some of the kids knew him and started making deals. There was nothing I could do. Are you sure you're okay?"

"Yes, I'm calling in at Alice's for some books."

"Go on, then. I'll wait here for you." He grinned, ruefully. "I'm dodging the press – off to stay with my aunt in Leeds till things blow over. I really am sorry about last night, you know."

"Yes." I looked across the field. There was nothing, now.

"I'll get the books."

"I'll wait for you."

"Suit yourself."

I crossed the track. The door was ajar. I knocked. No answer. I knocked again. "Go in," he called.

"She's probably deaf." I waited a few seconds, then pushed the door open and went in.

She was sitting in her battered armchair, and at first I thought she was sleeping, but she was not. The vigil of the Hazelbornes was over, and daft Alice had slipped away when nobody was looking.

Thirty-Five

THINGS DON'T CEASE TO BE, just because we hide them in the earth. Pit Field taught the village that, and what with that, and the panic, and the publicity, NERDS had no choice but to withdraw. We had a bit of a party to celebrate. We had it at Mabel's, and there was supposed to be just the seven of us but I think Alice came too. I felt her there, and that's reasonable, because people don't cease to be, either.

She left me her cottage. It was in a letter she wrote weeks ago, so she must have known the place wasn't about to be pulled down. She must have had a fair idea of what was going to happen to her, too. After NERDS left and we packed up camp, Mum and I moved in. Mum can't face going home, you see. Not yet anyway. I guess once you find your own space it's hard to go back. I visit Dad nearly every day, and he's got his space all right.

The others have gone home, but I think of them all

the time. We're sisters now – Mabel, Jan, Cathy, Midge, Kerry and me. Forever. Mum too, I suppose. When I told Maudlyn she said, "If your mum's your sister, someone's going to end up in jail." But that's just Maudlyn.

I see Tim at school and we say hi, but that's as far as it goes. I don't fall apart anymore when he's near me, so I guess he was just a crush.

The vicar came to Pit Field the other day and performed a re-consecration ceremony at the grave. Tim's dad got up a subscription round the village to erect a stone. It says

"Erected by the people of Apton Magna to the memory of villagers who perished in the plague of 1349, and of our sister, Alice Hazelborne, who watched over them."

I cried when I read it. They're landscaping the field, too, and rumour has it that old Ogden put up most of the money himself. When I remember how he wound down his window and shouted at us that day on the barricade, I find it hard to believe.

An amazing thing happened at school the other day, too. When we trooped in for assembly, Amanda Lawrence was up on the platform. I thought she must be in really bad trouble, but it turned out to be exactly the opposite. The head stood with one hand resting on Amanda's shoulder and told the whole school how, in the midst of what he called the crisis in Apton Magna, while everybody else was intent upon putting as much distance as possible between himself and the village, Amanda Lawrence walked there from Bradford to volunteer for work at the hard-pressed cottage hospital, believing that by doing so, she was placing herself in the most appalling danger.

I don't know. A few weeks ago I thought I was getting it all sorted out. Right and wrong. Goodies and baddies. All that. Now I'm not so sure. Maybe there aren't any goodies or baddies – just people, doing the best they know how and screwing other people up in the process.

Anyway, I dreamed again last night. In my dream I walked over the earth and it was mostly green. I saw clear skies with birds, and fish in crystal waters, and though I met many different sorts of people, they were all my sisters and my brothers. I had to wake up, of course, but that's not the end of it. It never is when I dream.

REMEMBRANCE OF THE SUN
Kate Gilmore

In a country embittered by the Shah's oppressive regime, romance must take second place to revolution, and Shaheen is prepared to sacrifice his musical talents, his plans for a college education in America, his love for Jill, and, if necessary, his life. Set in the turmoil of Iran before the revolution, this is at once a touching romance and a fascinating account of two young people from very different backgrounds torn between love and political ideals.

I CAN'T STAND LOSING
Gene Kemp

Patrick Gates is trying very hard to be positive but living at 17 Constance Place makes it pretty difficult. The Gates family are, in Patrick's own words, a bunch of no-hopers, excepting himself and Mum who somehow keep them all going. Then comes the memorable day when Mum packs her bags and says she's off to Greenham Common . . .

MADAME DOUBTFIRE
Anne Fine

Lydia, Christopher and Natalie are used to domestic turmoil and have been torn between their warring parents ever since the divorce. But all that changes when their mother takes on a most unusual cleaning lady. Despite her extraordinary appearance, Madame Doubtfire turns out to be a talented and efficient housekeeper and for a short time at least the arrangement is a resounding success. But as the children soon discover, there's more to Madame Doubtfire than domestic talents . . .

THE TWISTED WINDOW
Lois Duncan

Tracy can *feel* the new boy, Brad, looking at her. He's handsome enough and charming – but there's something about him that's rather sinister. Even so, she could never have known how dangerous he really was, or that she was destined to be part of his twisted plans. A taut and unusual thriller.

BUDDY'S SONG
Nigel Hinton

Buddy's in a bad way. His dad, Terry, is in prison; people are being pretty nasty at school; and his mum is busy with her new job. He feels lonely and confused, until one day he decides to learn how to play an old guitar and quickly discovers why his dad loves rock 'n' roll so much. There's excitement, happiness and a way of expressing feelings in music. And there's the chance to dream – of girls, friends and a happy future. But he finds out that his dad has dreams too – which could go out of control and threaten what Buddy wants most. A terrific sequel to *Buddy*.

A BUNDLE OF NERVES
Joan Aiken

Joan Aiken shuffles the surface of the everyday and deals out a handful of stories that range from the weird and fantastic to the ghostly and sharply macabre, but all of which are firmly rooted in the plausible. An excellent collection from a compelling writer.